# ACTION LAB ENTERTAINMENT PROUDLY PRESENTS

# Vamplets

## THIS BOOK IS BASED ON ORIGINAL CHARACTERS. STORY AND ART BY GAYLE MIDDLETON

### WRITTEN BY

## GAYLE MIDDLETON
## &
## DAVE DWONCH

### ART BY

## AMANDA CORONADO
## WITH
## BILL BLANKENSHIP

### EDITED BY: DARYL BANNER AND BETH DOBIN-COLLAKU

BRYAN SEATON - PUBLISHER
KEVIN FREEMAN - PRESIDENT
SHAWN PRYOR - VP DIGITAL MEDIA
SHAWN GABBORIN - EDITOR IN CHIEF
DAVE DWONCH - CREATIVE DIRECTOR
JASON MARTIN - EDITOR
CHAD CICCONI - BASS PLAYER IN THE MUSICAL MAYHEM SOCIETY
COLLEEN BOYD - ASSOCIATE EDITOR
JAMAL IGLE & KELLY DALE - DIRECTORS OF MARKETING

# CHAPTER 5

## "POTIONS, PREDICTIONS, AND PERIL"

WRITTEN BY GAYLE MIDDLETON AND DAVE DWONCH
DRAWN BY AMANDA CORONADO
COLOR ART BY BILL BLANKENSHIP
LETTERED BY DAVE DWONCH

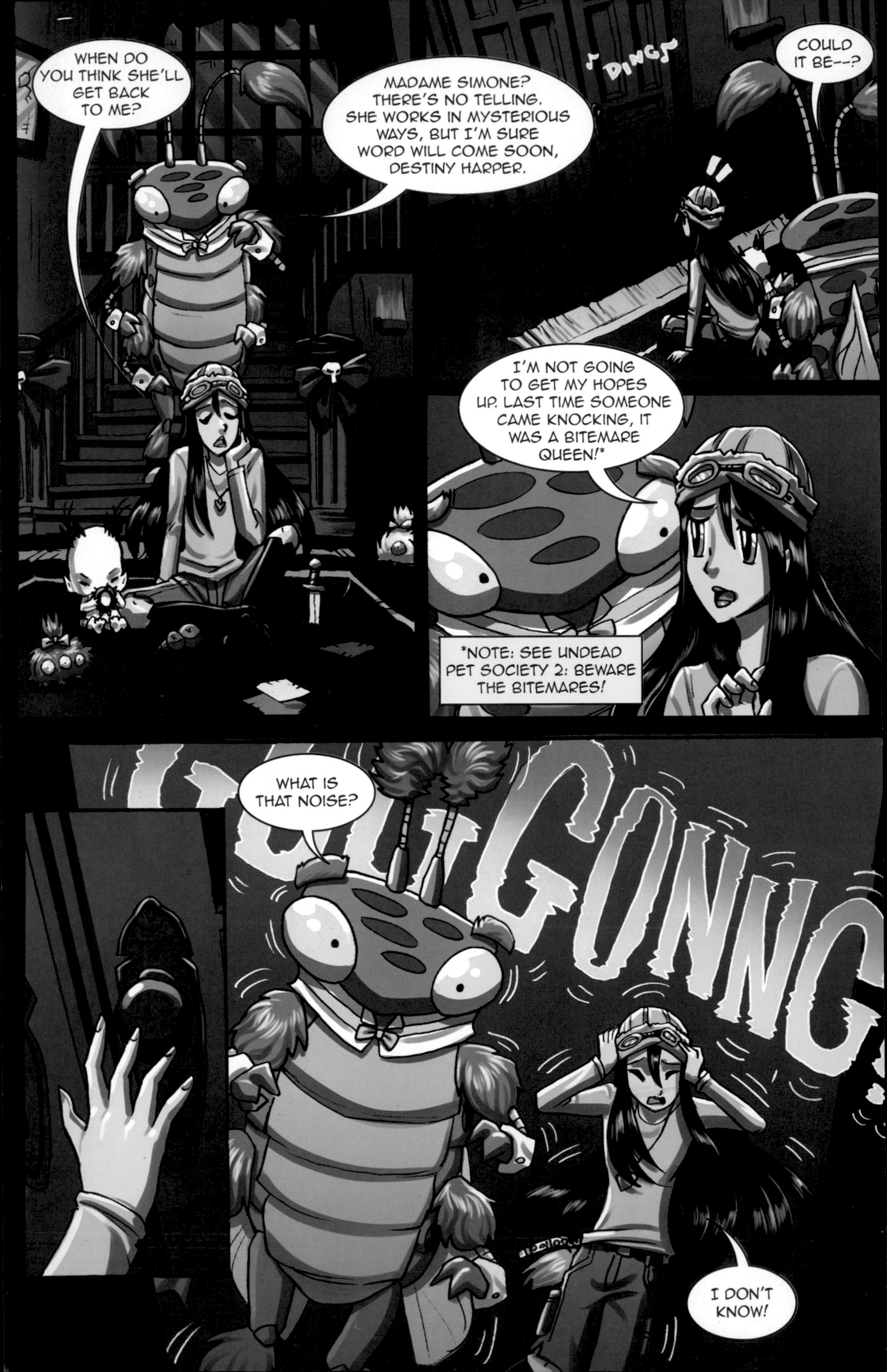
WHEN DO YOU THINK SHE'LL GET BACK TO ME?
MADAME SIMONE? THERE'S NO TELLING. SHE WORKS IN MYSTERIOUS WAYS, BUT I'M SURE WORD WILL COME SOON, DESTINY HARPER.
DING
COULD IT BE--?
I'M NOT GOING TO GET MY HOPES UP. LAST TIME SOMEONE CAME KNOCKING, IT WAS A BITEMARE QUEEN!*
*NOTE: SEE UNDEAD PET SOCIETY 2: BEWARE THE BITEMARES!
GONNG
WHAT IS THAT NOISE?
I DON'T KNOW!

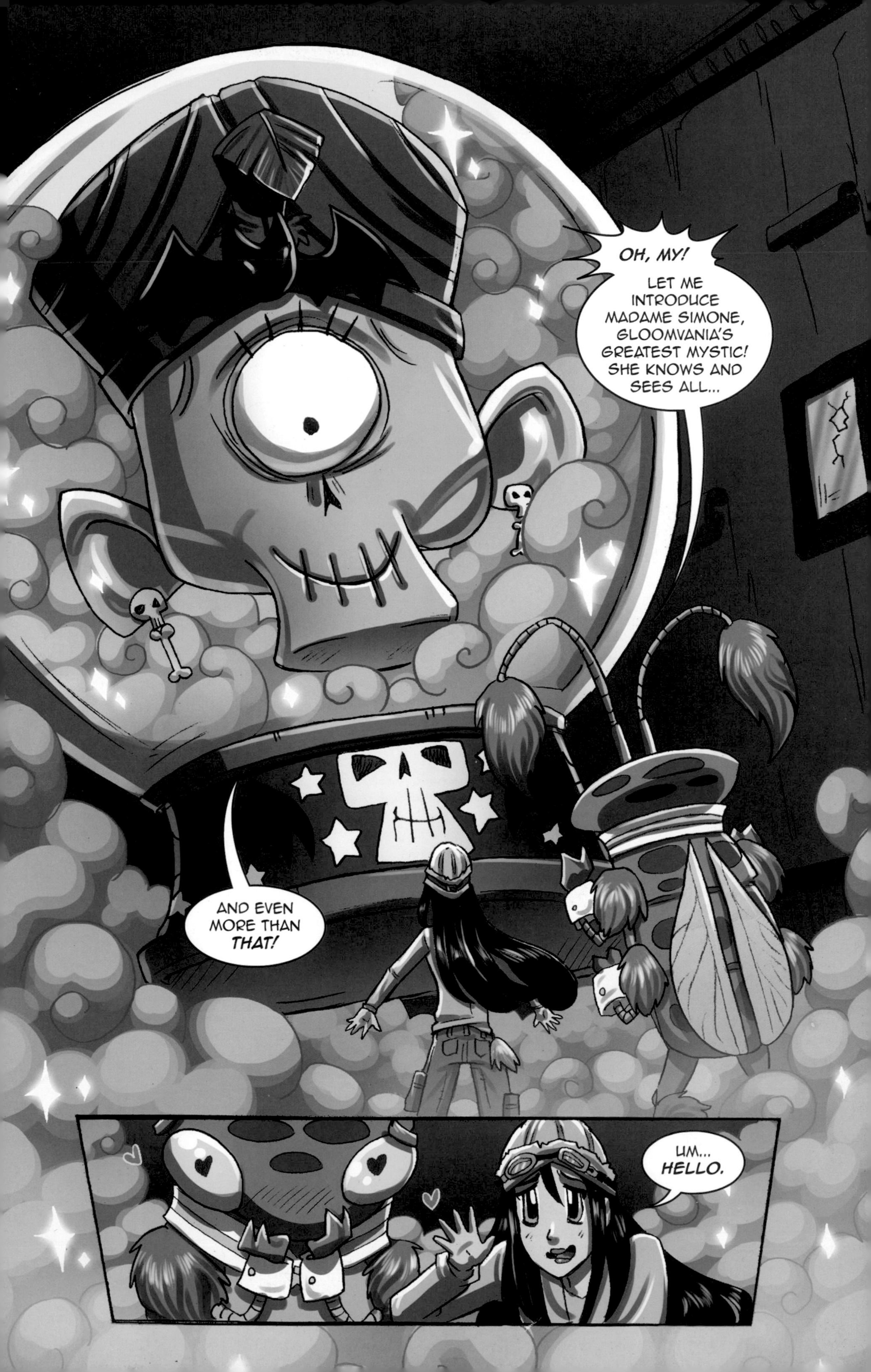
OH, MY!
LET ME INTRODUCE MADAME SIMONE, GLOOMVANIA'S GREATEST MYSTIC! SHE KNOWS AND SEES ALL...
AND EVEN MORE THAN THAT!
UM... HELLO.

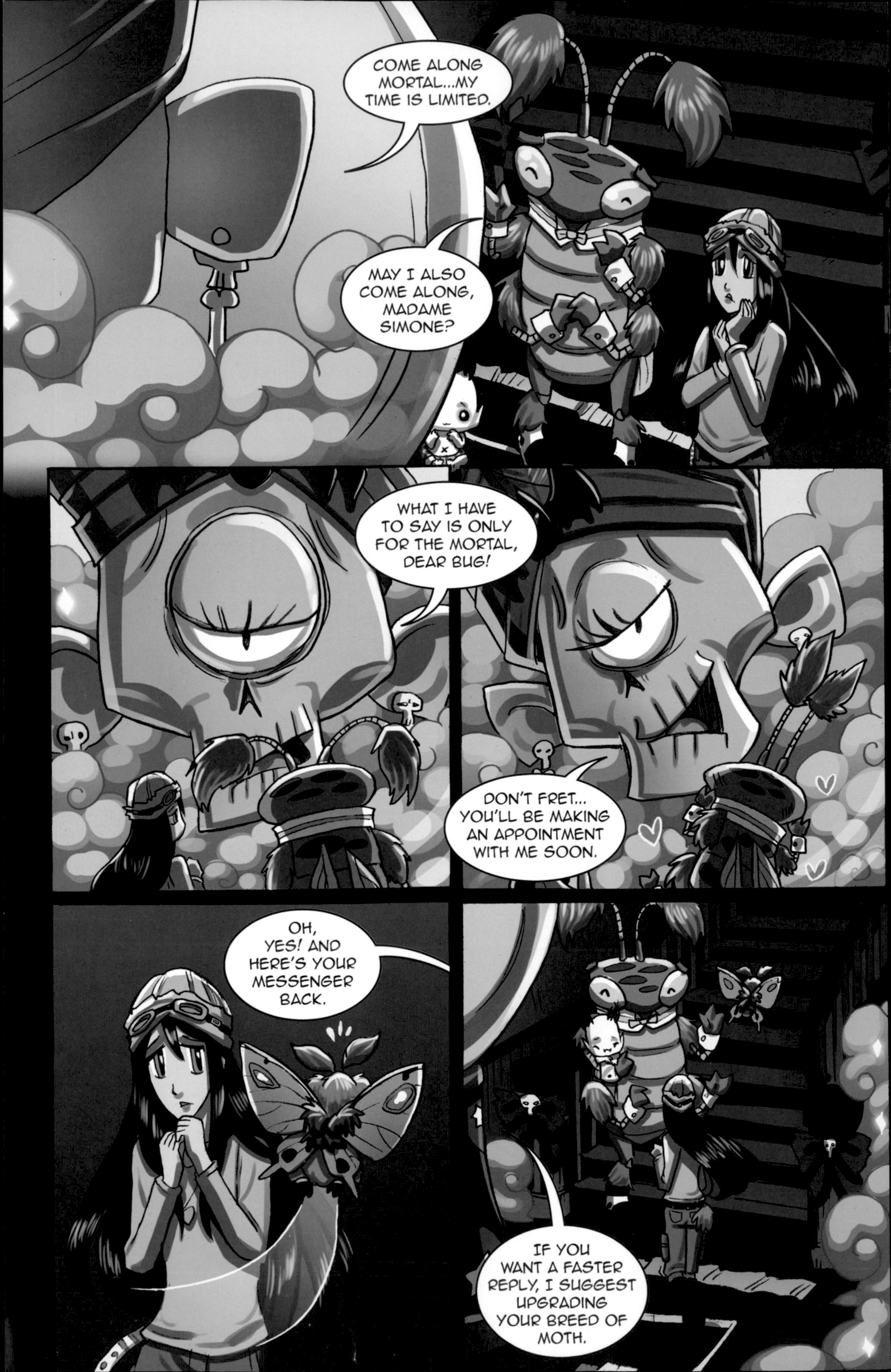
COME ALONG MORTAL...MY TIME IS LIMITED.
MAY I ALSO COME ALONG, MADAME SIMONE?
WHAT I HAVE TO SAY IS ONLY FOR THE MORTAL, DEAR BUG!
DON'T FRET... YOU'LL BE MAKING AN APPOINTMENT WITH ME SOON.
OH, YES! AND HERE'S YOUR MESSENGER BACK.
IF YOU WANT A FASTER REPLY, I SUGGEST UPGRADING YOUR BREED OF MOTH.

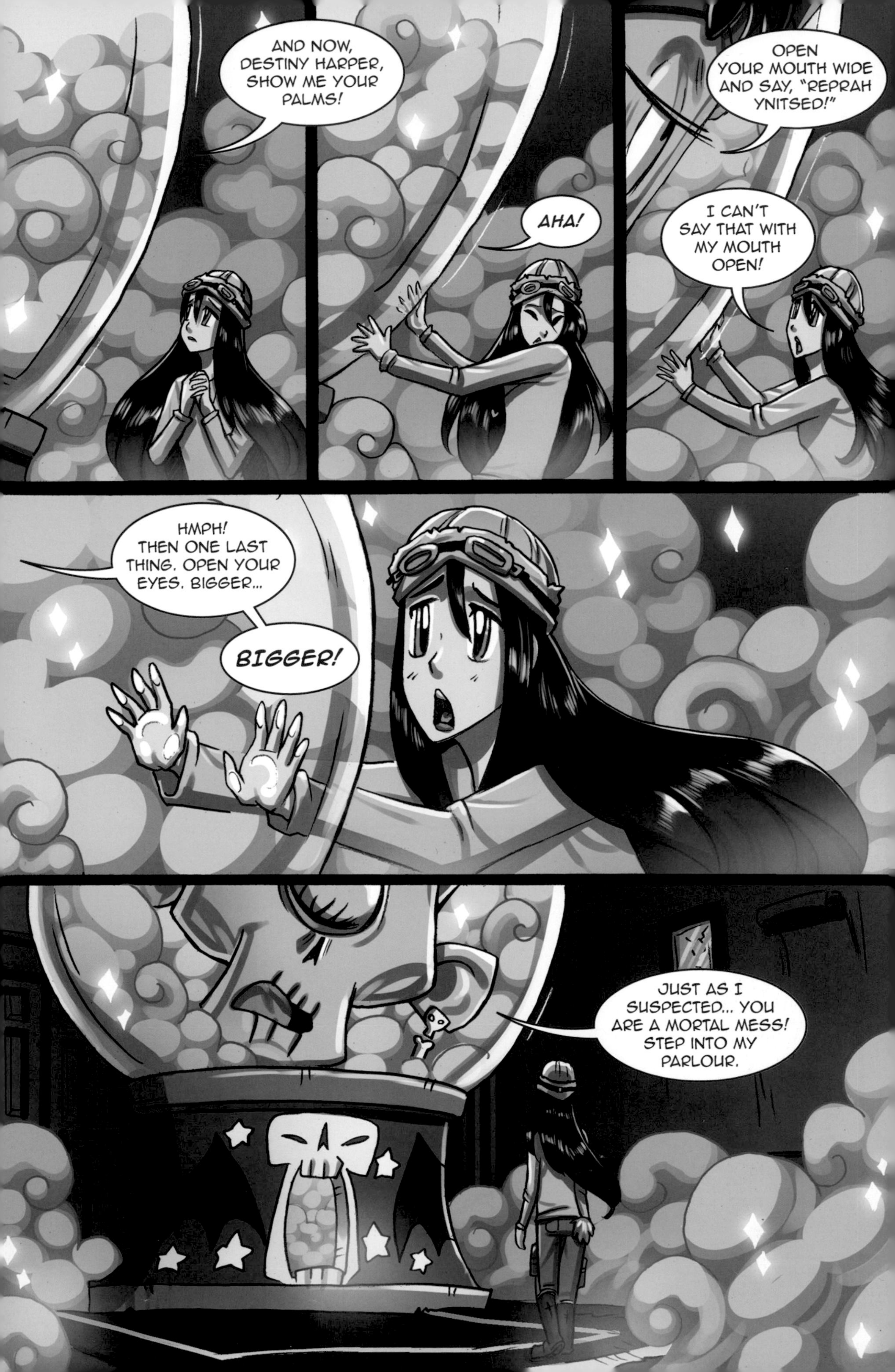
AND NOW, DESTINY HARPER, SHOW ME YOUR PALMS!
AHA!
OPEN YOUR MOUTH WIDE AND SAY, "REPRAH YNITSED!"
I CAN'T SAY THAT WITH MY MOUTH OPEN!
HMPH! THEN ONE LAST THING. OPEN YOUR EYES. BIGGER...
BIGGER!
JUST AS I SUSPECTED... YOU ARE A MORTAL MESS! STEP INTO MY PARLOUR.

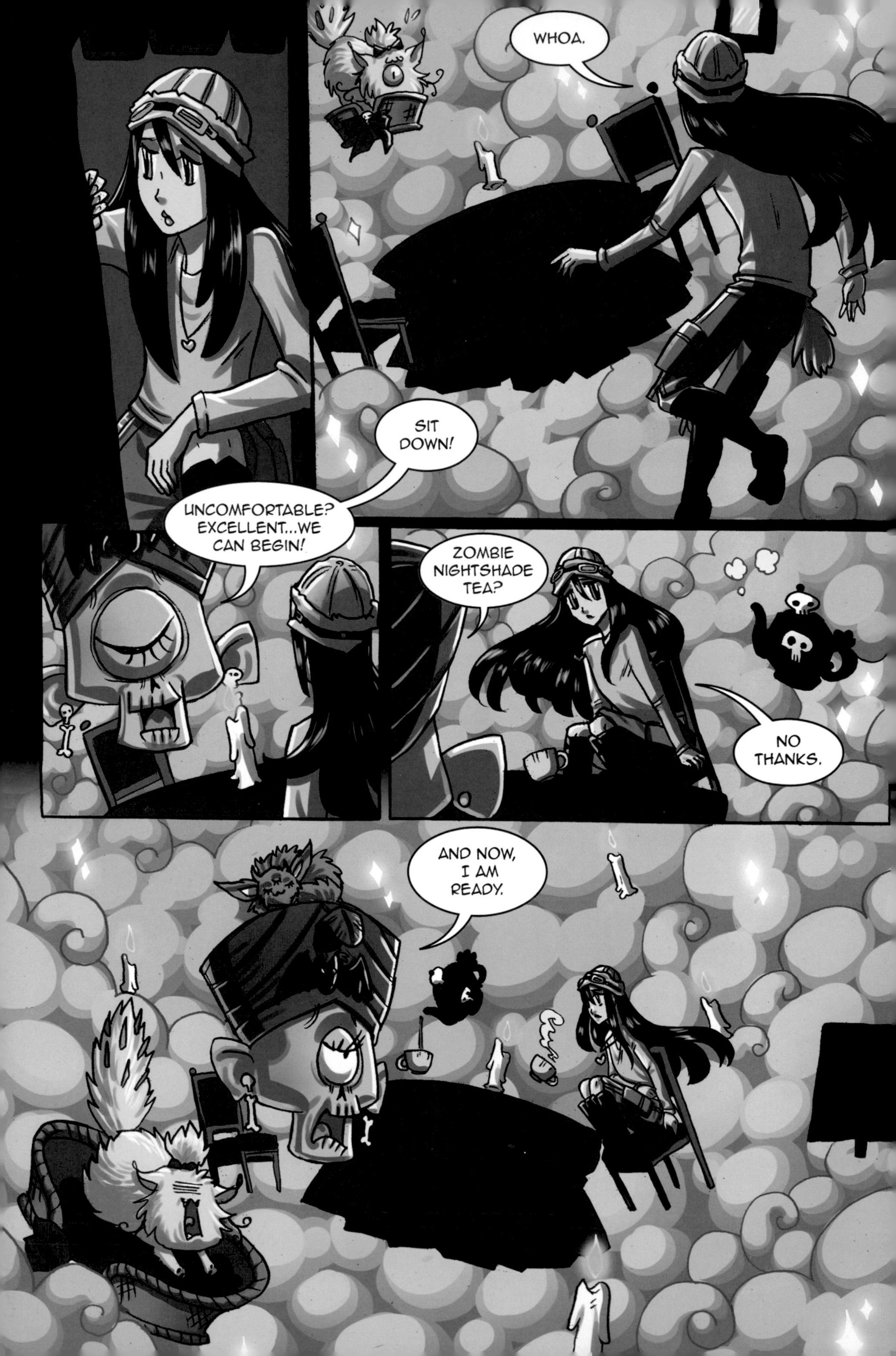
WHOA.
SIT DOWN!
UNCOMFORTABLE? EXCELLENT...WE CAN BEGIN!
ZOMBIE NIGHTSHADE TEA?
NO THANKS.
AND NOW, I AM READY.

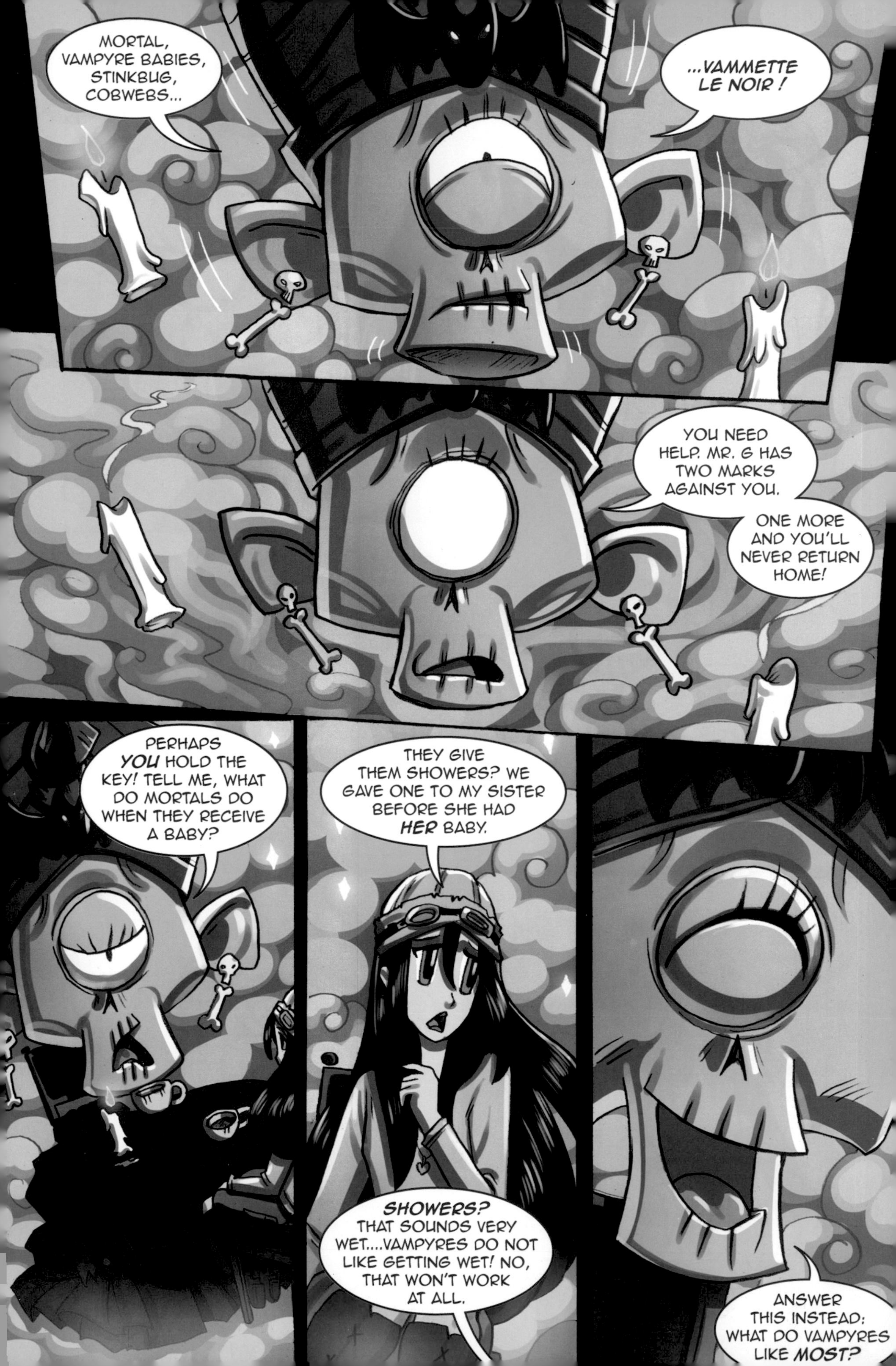
MORTAL, VAMPYRE BABIES, STINKBUG, COBWEBS...
...VAMMETTE LE NOIR!
YOU NEED HELP. MR. G HAS TWO MARKS AGAINST YOU.
ONE MORE AND YOU'LL NEVER RETURN HOME!
PERHAPS *YOU* HOLD THE KEY! TELL ME, WHAT DO MORTALS DO WHEN THEY RECEIVE A BABY?
THEY GIVE THEM SHOWERS? WE GAVE ONE TO MY SISTER BEFORE SHE HAD *HER* BABY.
*SHOWERS?* THAT SOUNDS VERY WET....VAMPYRES DO NOT LIKE GETTING WET! NO, THAT WON'T WORK AT ALL.
ANSWER THIS INSTEAD: WHAT DO VAMPYRES LIKE *MOST?*

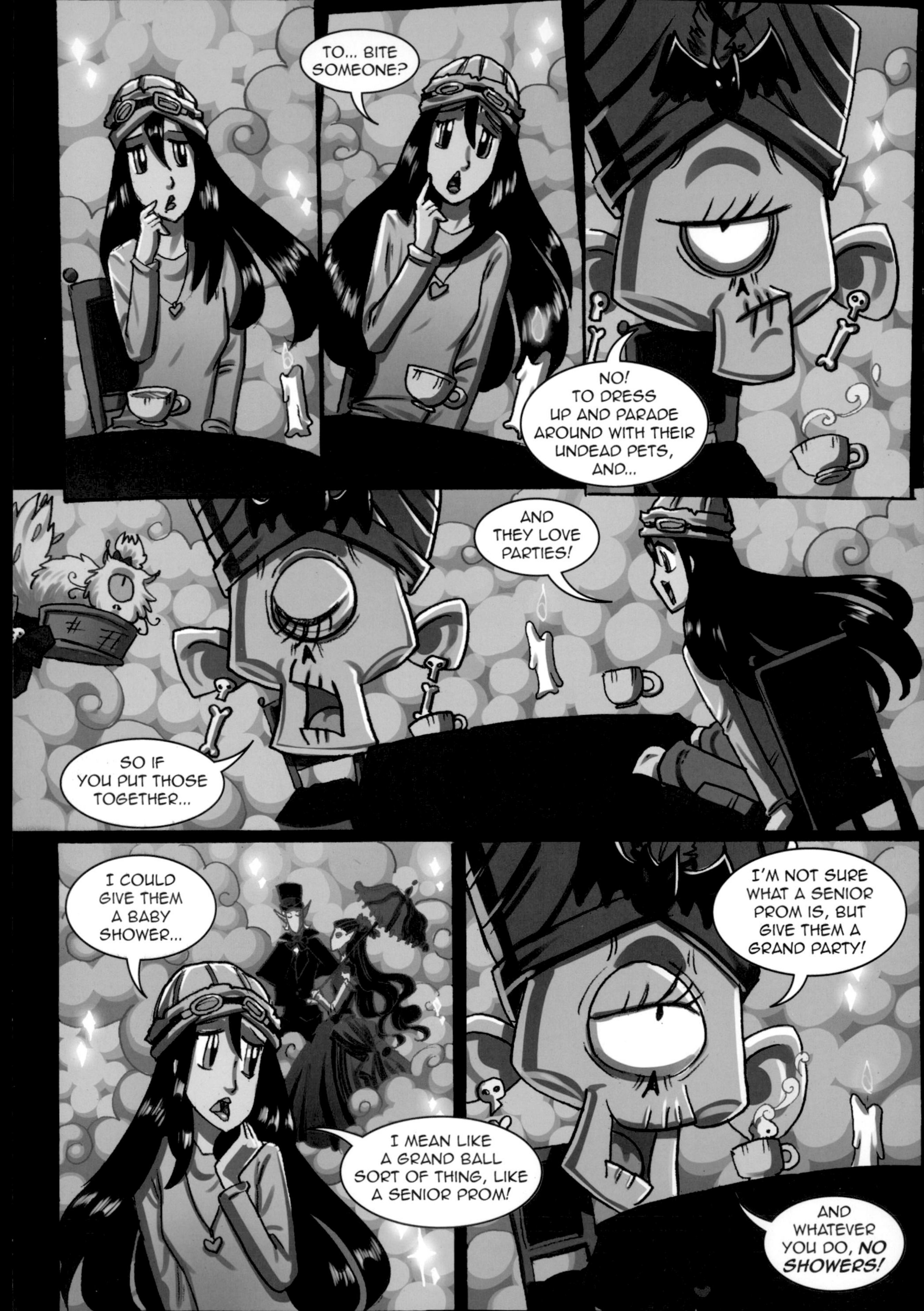
TO... BITE SOMEONE?
NO! TO DRESS UP AND PARADE AROUND WITH THEIR UNDEAD PETS, AND...
AND THEY LOVE PARTIES!
SO IF YOU PUT THOSE TOGETHER...
I COULD GIVE THEM A BABY SHOWER...
I MEAN LIKE A GRAND BALL SORT OF THING, LIKE A SENIOR PROM!
I'M NOT SURE WHAT A SENIOR PROM IS, BUT GIVE THEM A GRAND PARTY!
AND WHATEVER YOU DO, **NO SHOWERS!**

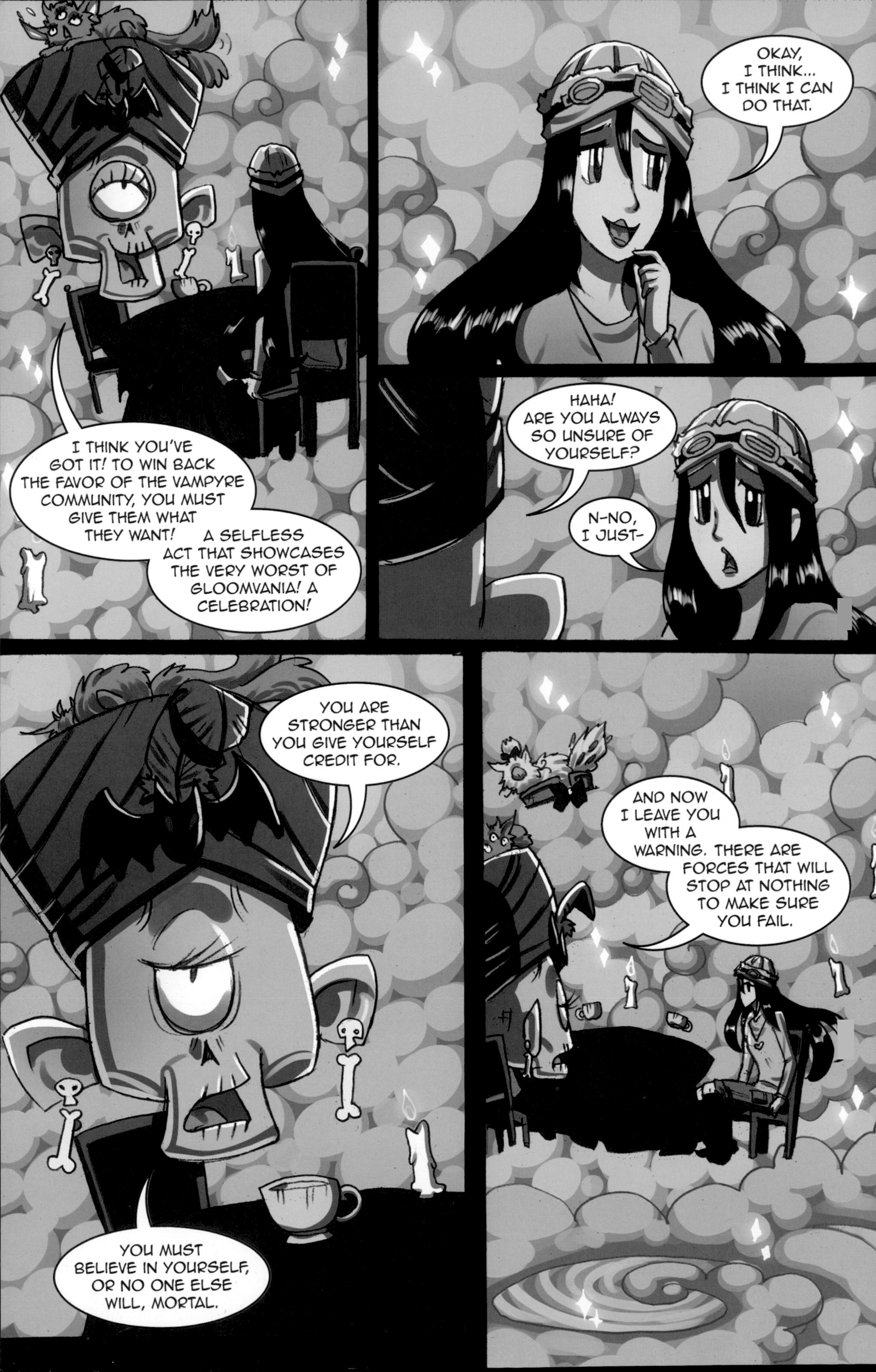
I THINK YOU'VE GOT IT! TO WIN BACK THE FAVOR OF THE VAMPYRE COMMUNITY, YOU MUST GIVE THEM WHAT THEY WANT!
A SELFLESS ACT THAT SHOWCASES THE VERY WORST OF GLOOMVANIA! A CELEBRATION!
OKAY, I THINK... I THINK I CAN DO THAT.
HAHA! ARE YOU ALWAYS SO UNSURE OF YOURSELF?
N-NO, I JUST-
YOU ARE STRONGER THAN YOU GIVE YOURSELF CREDIT FOR.
YOU MUST BELIEVE IN YOURSELF, OR NO ONE ELSE WILL, MORTAL.
AND NOW I LEAVE YOU WITH A WARNING. THERE ARE FORCES THAT WILL STOP AT NOTHING TO MAKE SURE YOU FAIL.

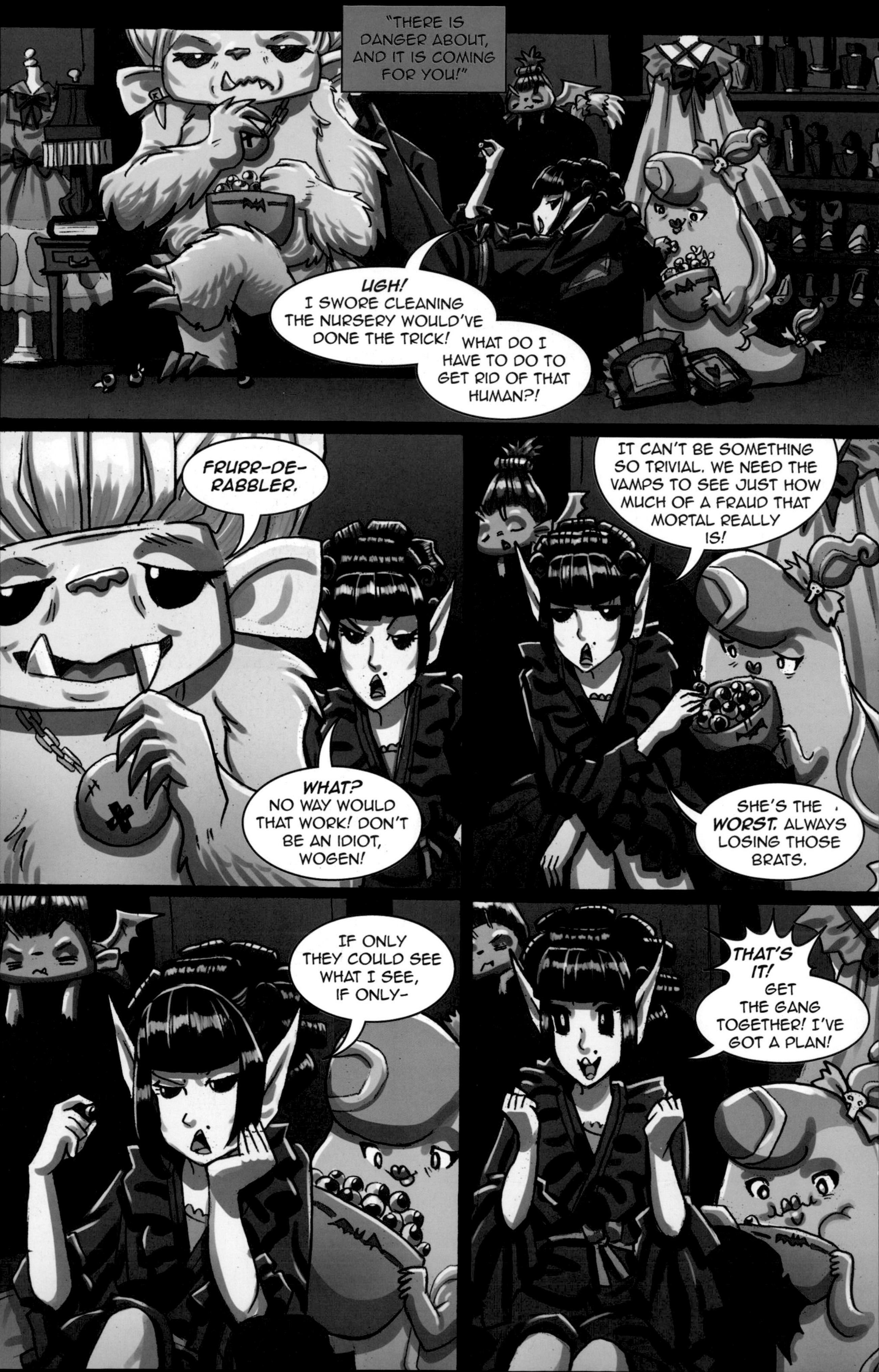
"THERE IS DANGER ABOUT, AND IT IS COMING FOR YOU!"
UGH! I SWORE CLEANING THE NURSERY WOULD'VE DONE THE TRICK!
WHAT DO I HAVE TO DO TO GET RID OF THAT HUMAN?!
FRURR-DE-RABBLER.
WHAT? NO WAY WOULD THAT WORK! DON'T BE AN IDIOT, WOGEN!
IT CAN'T BE SOMETHING SO TRIVIAL. WE NEED THE VAMPS TO SEE JUST HOW MUCH OF A FRAUD THAT MORTAL REALLY IS!
SHE'S THE WORST. ALWAYS LOSING THOSE BRATS.
IF ONLY THEY COULD SEE WHAT I SEE, IF ONLY-
THAT'S IT! GET THE GANG TOGETHER! I'VE GOT A PLAN!

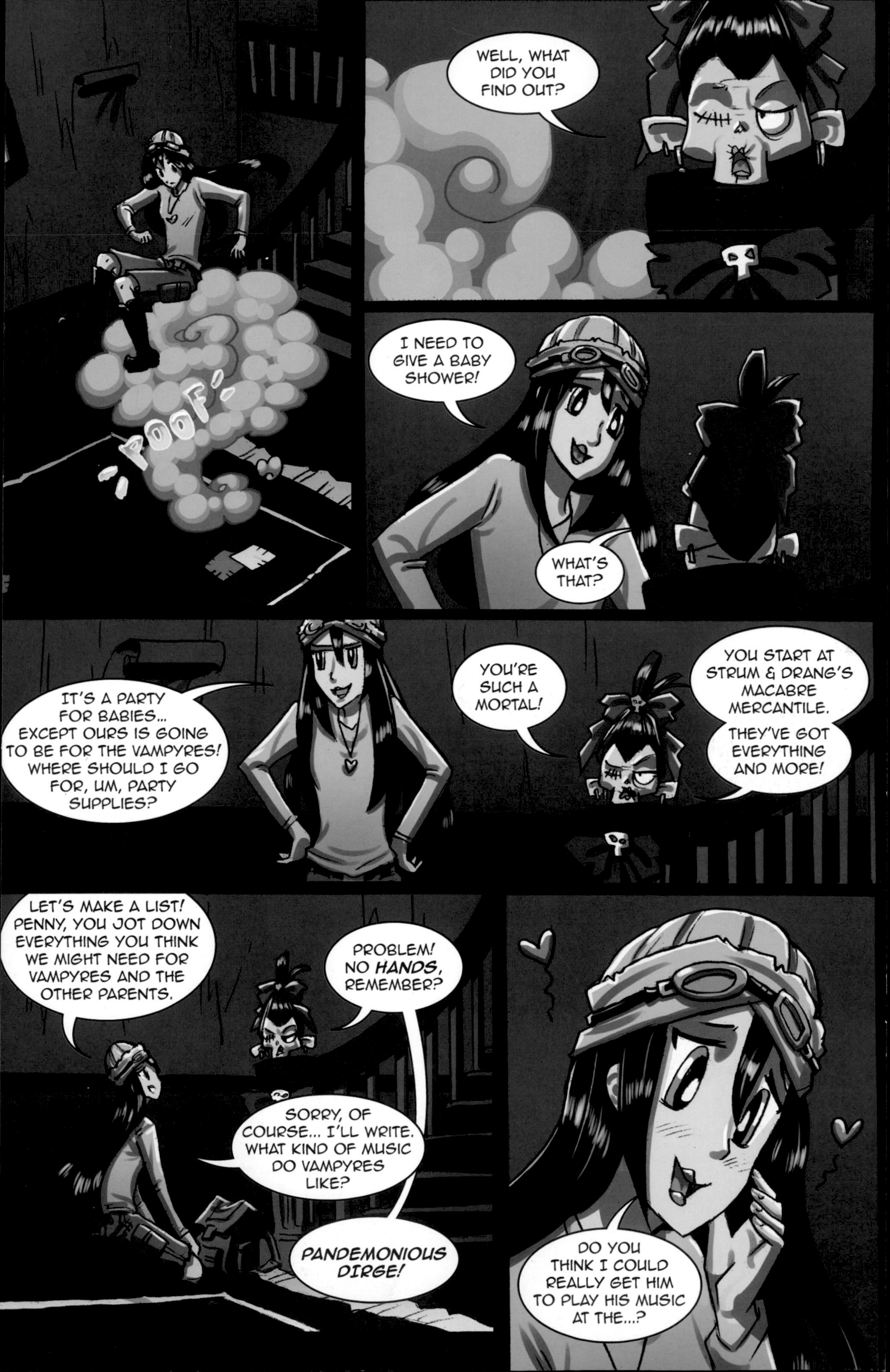
POOF!
WELL, WHAT DID YOU FIND OUT?
I NEED TO GIVE A BABY SHOWER!
WHAT'S THAT?
IT'S A PARTY FOR BABIES... EXCEPT OURS IS GOING TO BE FOR THE VAMPYRES! WHERE SHOULD I GO FOR, UM, PARTY SUPPLIES?
YOU'RE SUCH A MORTAL!
YOU START AT STRUM & DRANG'S MACABRE MERCANTILE.
THEY'VE GOT EVERYTHING AND MORE!
LET'S MAKE A LIST! PENNY, YOU JOT DOWN EVERYTHING YOU THINK WE MIGHT NEED FOR VAMPYRES AND THE OTHER PARENTS.
PROBLEM! NO *HANDS*, REMEMBER?
SORRY, OF COURSE... I'LL WRITE. WHAT KIND OF MUSIC DO VAMPYRES LIKE?
*PANDEMONIOUS DIRGE!*
DO YOU THINK I COULD REALLY GET HIM TO PLAY HIS MUSIC AT THE...?

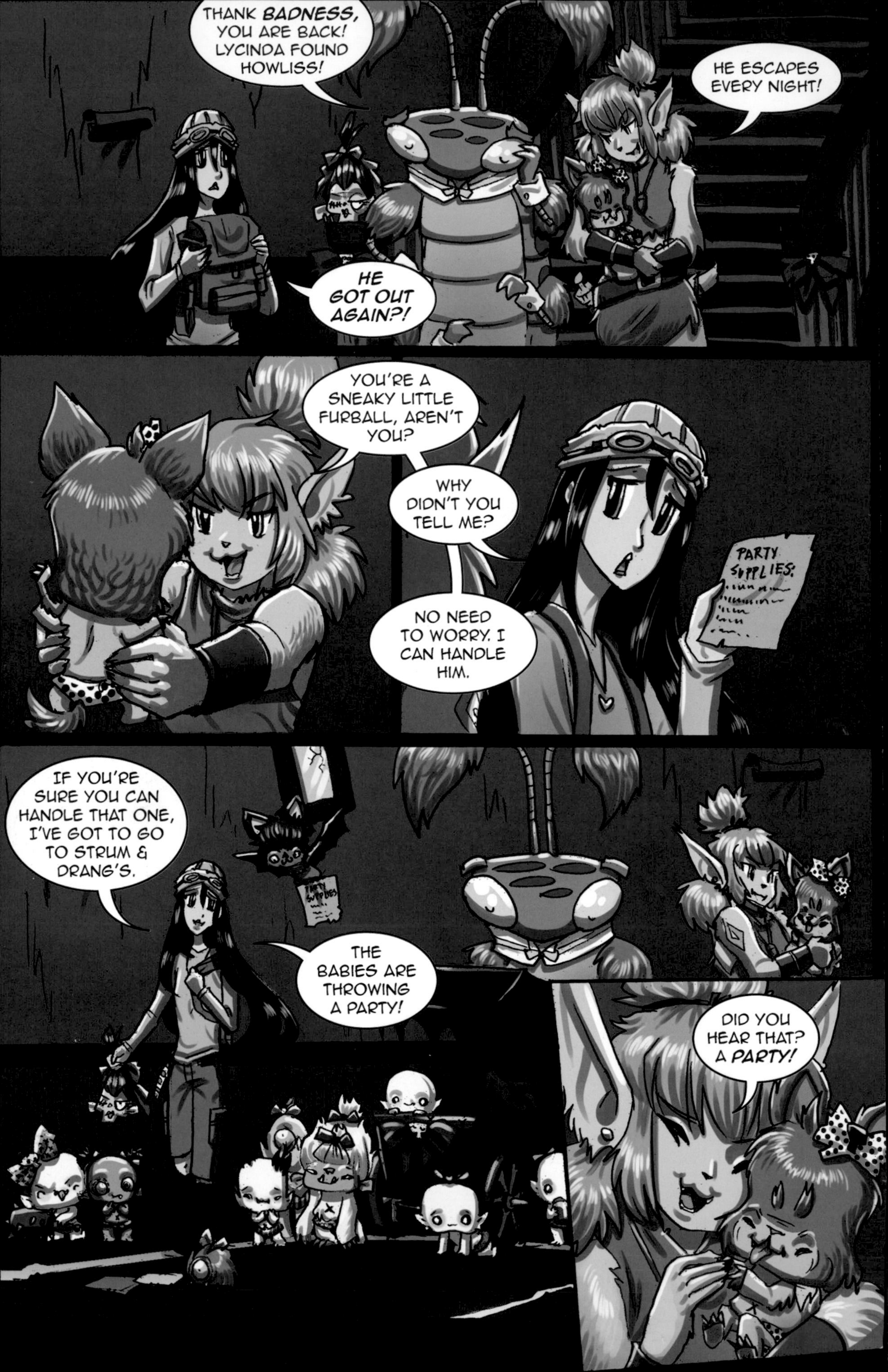
THANK BADNESS, YOU ARE BACK! LYCINDA FOUND HOWLISS!
HE ESCAPES EVERY NIGHT!
HE GOT OUT AGAIN?!
YOU'RE A SNEAKY LITTLE FURBALL, AREN'T YOU?
WHY DIDN'T YOU TELL ME?
NO NEED TO WORRY. I CAN HANDLE HIM.
PARTY SUPPLIES:
IF YOU'RE SURE YOU CAN HANDLE THAT ONE, I'VE GOT TO GO TO STRUM & DRANG'S.
THE BABIES ARE THROWING A PARTY!
DID YOU HEAR THAT? A PARTY!

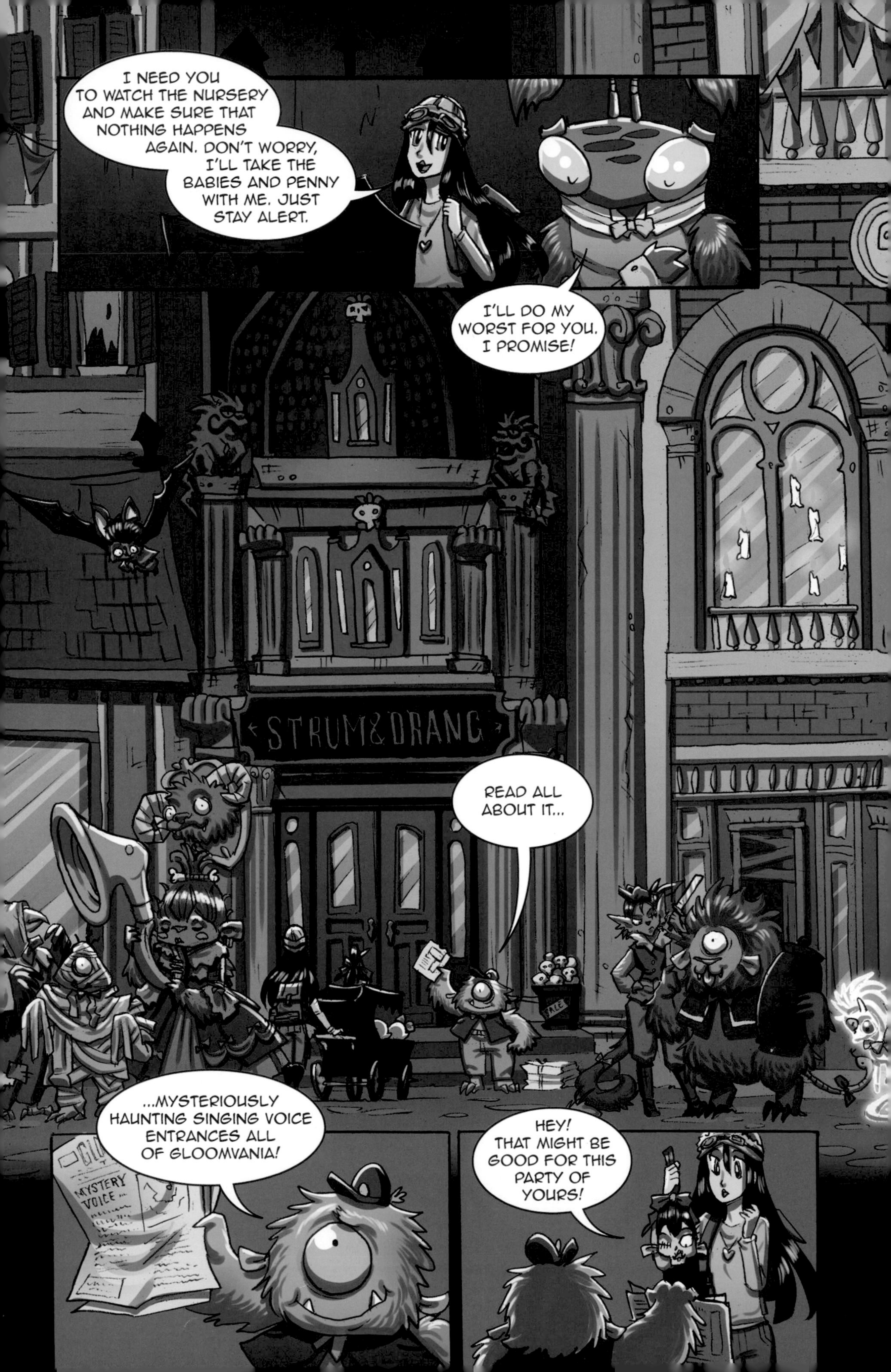
I NEED YOU TO WATCH THE NURSERY AND MAKE SURE THAT NOTHING HAPPENS AGAIN. DON'T WORRY, I'LL TAKE THE BABIES AND PENNY WITH ME. JUST STAY ALERT.
I'LL DO MY WORST FOR YOU. I PROMISE!
STRUM&DRANG
READ ALL ABOUT IT...
...MYSTERIOUSLY HAUNTING SINGING VOICE ENTRANCES ALL OF GLOOMVANIA!
MYSTERY VOICE...
HEY! THAT MIGHT BE GOOD FOR THIS PARTY OF YOURS!

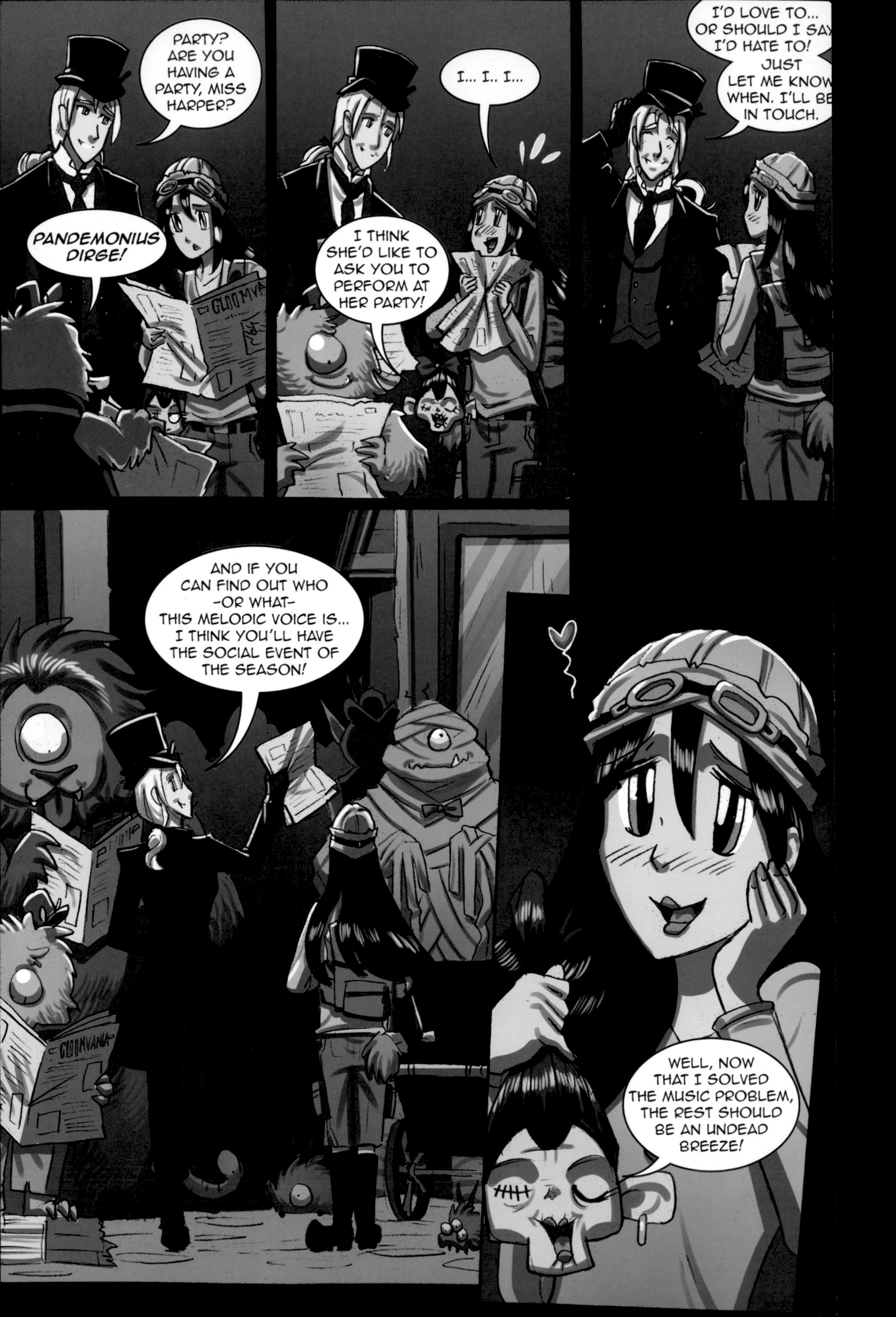
PARTY? ARE YOU HAVING A PARTY, MISS HARPER?
PANDEMONIUS DIRGE!
I... I.. I...
I THINK SHE'D LIKE TO ASK YOU TO PERFORM AT HER PARTY!
I'D LOVE TO... OR SHOULD I SAY I'D HATE TO! JUST LET ME KNOW WHEN. I'LL BE IN TOUCH.
AND IF YOU CAN FIND OUT WHO -OR WHAT- THIS MELODIC VOICE IS... I THINK YOU'LL HAVE THE SOCIAL EVENT OF THE SEASON!
WELL, NOW THAT I SOLVED THE MUSIC PROBLEM, THE REST SHOULD BE AN UNDEAD BREEZE!

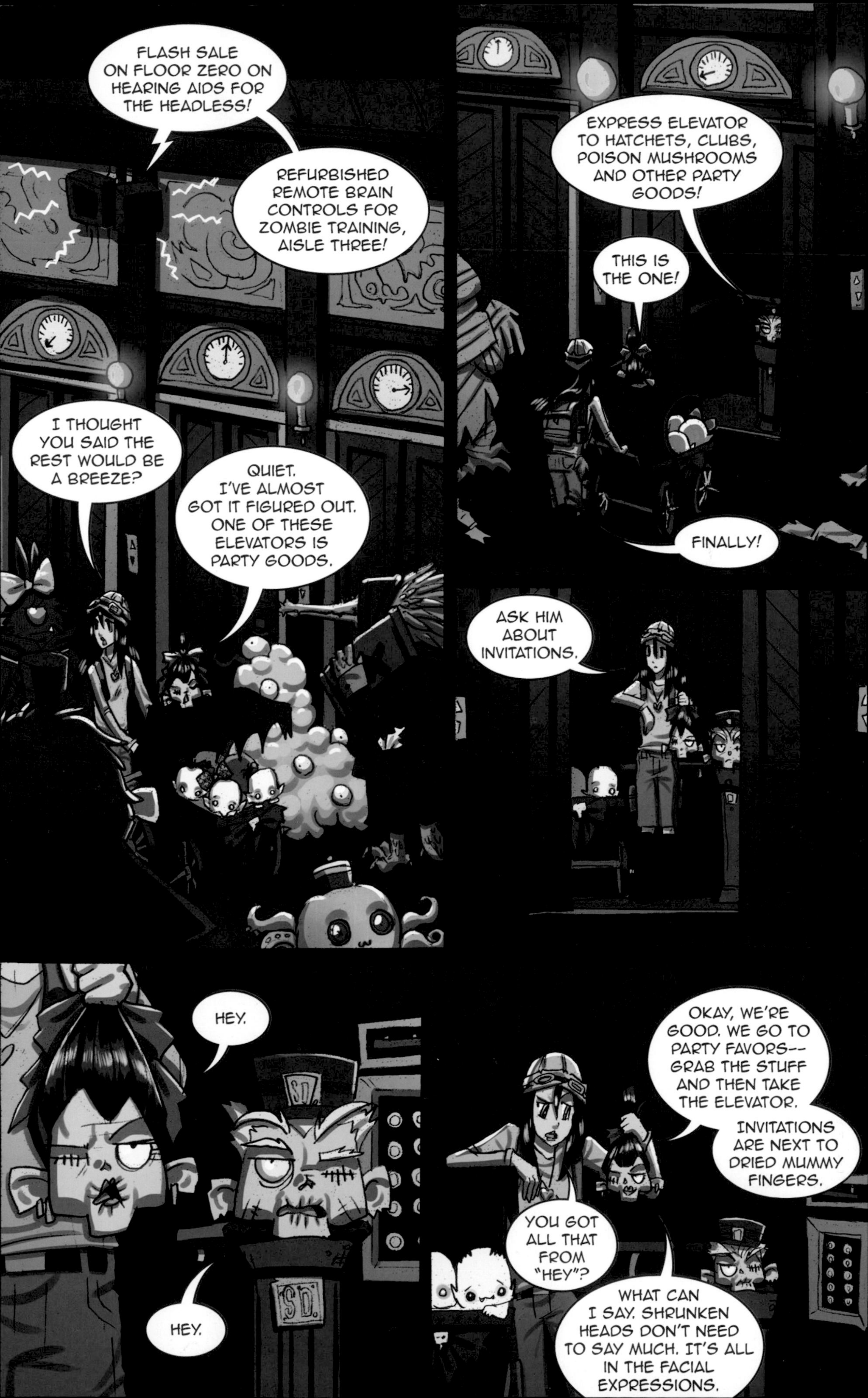
FLASH SALE ON FLOOR ZERO ON HEARING AIDS FOR THE HEADLESS!
REFURBISHED REMOTE BRAIN CONTROLS FOR ZOMBIE TRAINING, AISLE THREE!
I THOUGHT YOU SAID THE REST WOULD BE A BREEZE?
QUIET. I'VE ALMOST GOT IT FIGURED OUT. ONE OF THESE ELEVATORS IS PARTY GOODS.
EXPRESS ELEVATOR TO HATCHETS, CLUBS, POISON MUSHROOMS AND OTHER PARTY GOODS!
THIS IS THE ONE!
FINALLY!
ASK HIM ABOUT INVITATIONS.
HEY.
HEY.
OKAY, WE'RE GOOD. WE GO TO PARTY FAVORS-- GRAB THE STUFF AND THEN TAKE THE ELEVATOR.
INVITATIONS ARE NEXT TO DRIED MUMMY FINGERS.
YOU GOT ALL THAT FROM "HEY"?
WHAT CAN I SAY. SHRUNKEN HEADS DON'T NEED TO SAY MUCH. IT'S ALL IN THE FACIAL EXPRESSIONS.

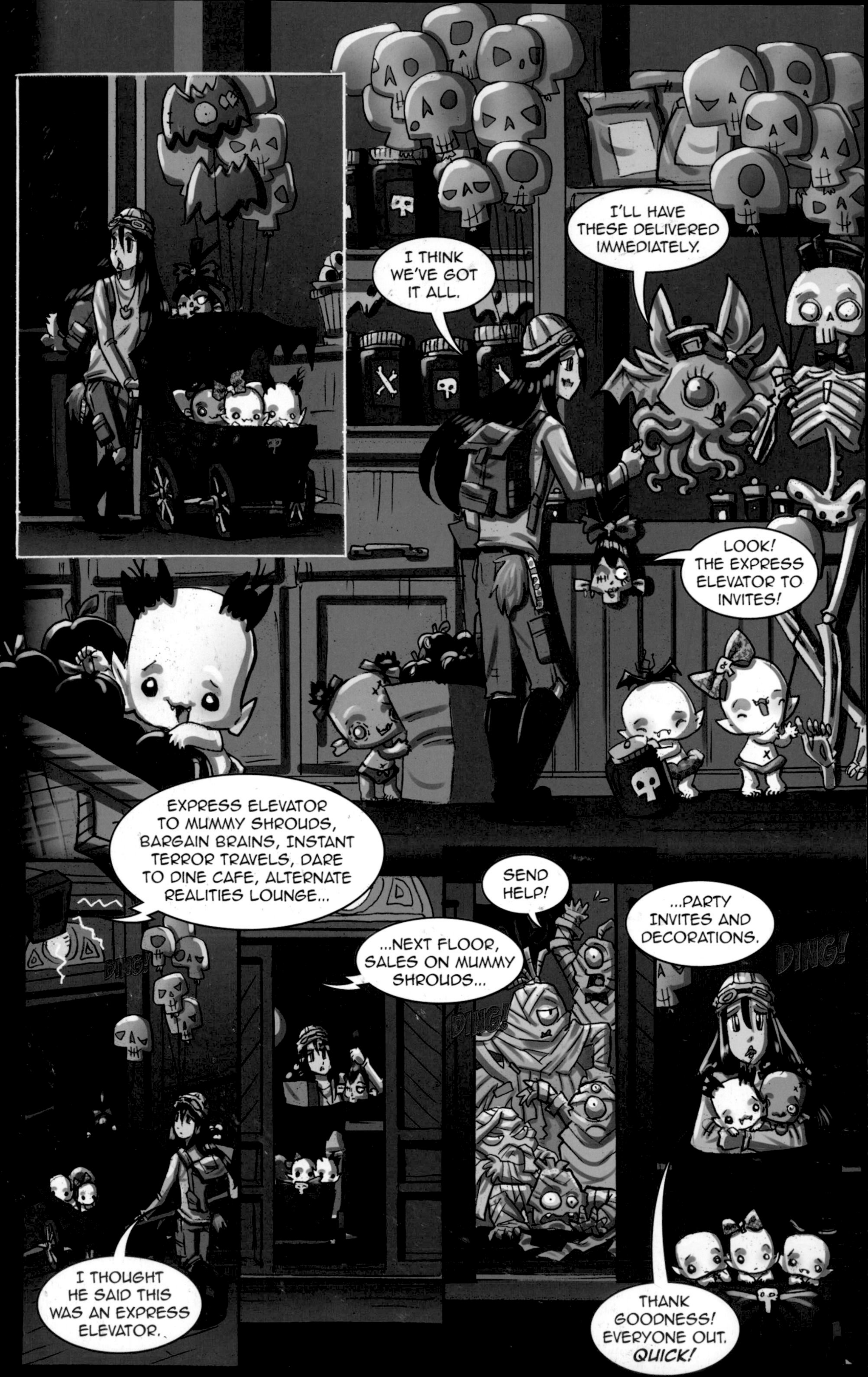
I THINK WE'VE GOT IT ALL.
I'LL HAVE THESE DELIVERED IMMEDIATELY.
LOOK! THE EXPRESS ELEVATOR TO INVITES!
EXPRESS ELEVATOR TO MUMMY SHROUDS, BARGAIN BRAINS, INSTANT TERROR TRAVELS, DARE TO DINE CAFE, ALTERNATE REALITIES LOUNGE...
DING!
...NEXT FLOOR, SALES ON MUMMY SHROUDS...
SEND HELP!
DING!
...PARTY INVITES AND DECORATIONS.
DING!
I THOUGHT HE SAID THIS WAS AN EXPRESS ELEVATOR.
THANK GOODNESS! EVERYONE OUT. QUICK!

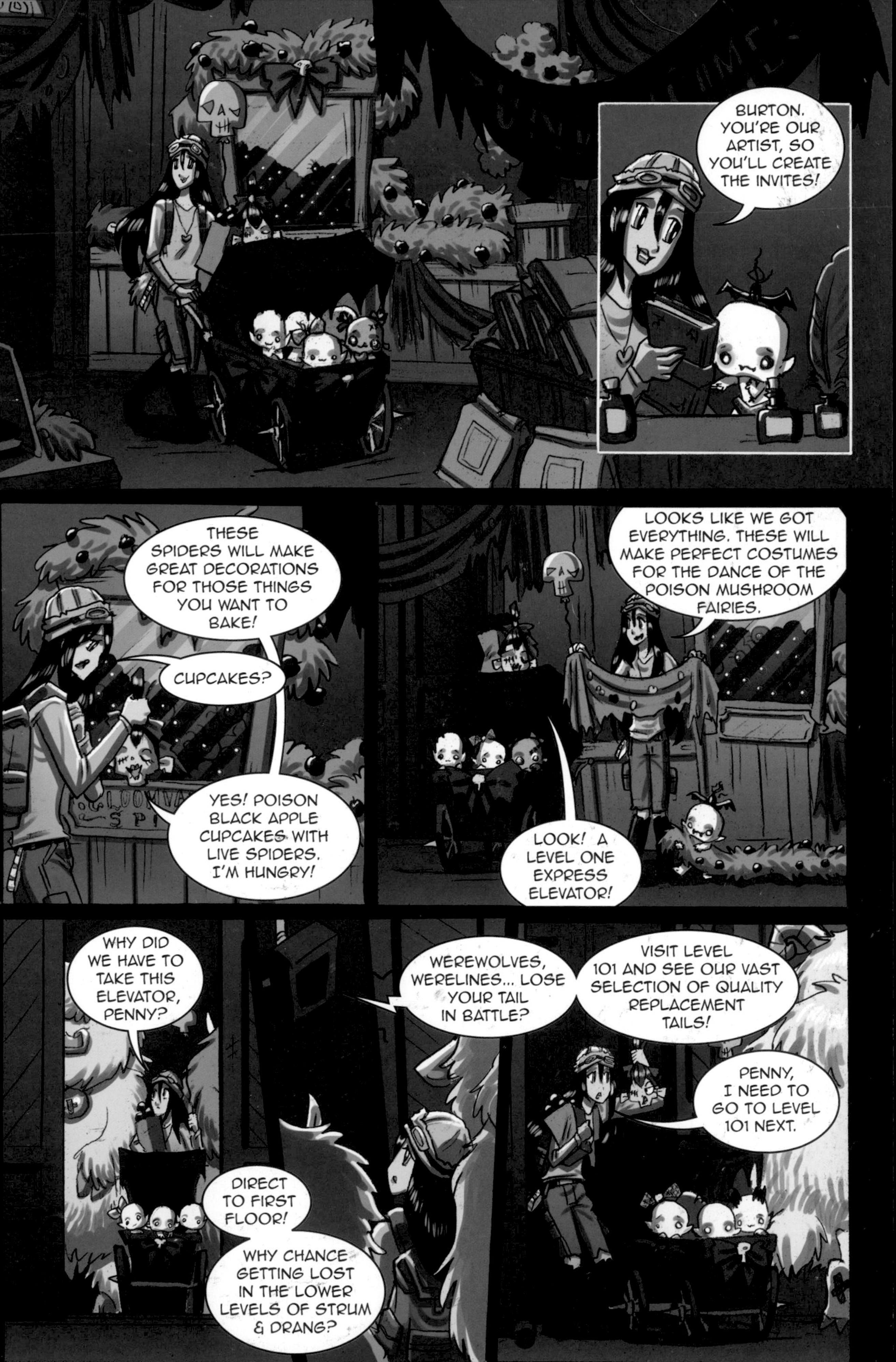
BURTON. YOU'RE OUR ARTIST, SO YOU'LL CREATE THE INVITES!
THESE SPIDERS WILL MAKE GREAT DECORATIONS FOR THOSE THINGS YOU WANT TO BAKE!
CUPCAKES?
YES! POISON BLACK APPLE CUPCAKES WITH LIVE SPIDERS. I'M HUNGRY!
LOOKS LIKE WE GOT EVERYTHING. THESE WILL MAKE PERFECT COSTUMES FOR THE DANCE OF THE POISON MUSHROOM FAIRIES.
LOOK! A LEVEL ONE EXPRESS ELEVATOR!
WHY DID WE HAVE TO TAKE THIS ELEVATOR, PENNY?
DIRECT TO FIRST FLOOR!
WHY CHANCE GETTING LOST IN THE LOWER LEVELS OF STRUM & DRANG?
WEREWOLVES, WERELINES... LOSE YOUR TAIL IN BATTLE?
VISIT LEVEL 101 AND SEE OUR VAST SELECTION OF QUALITY REPLACEMENT TAILS!
PENNY, I NEED TO GO TO LEVEL 101 NEXT.

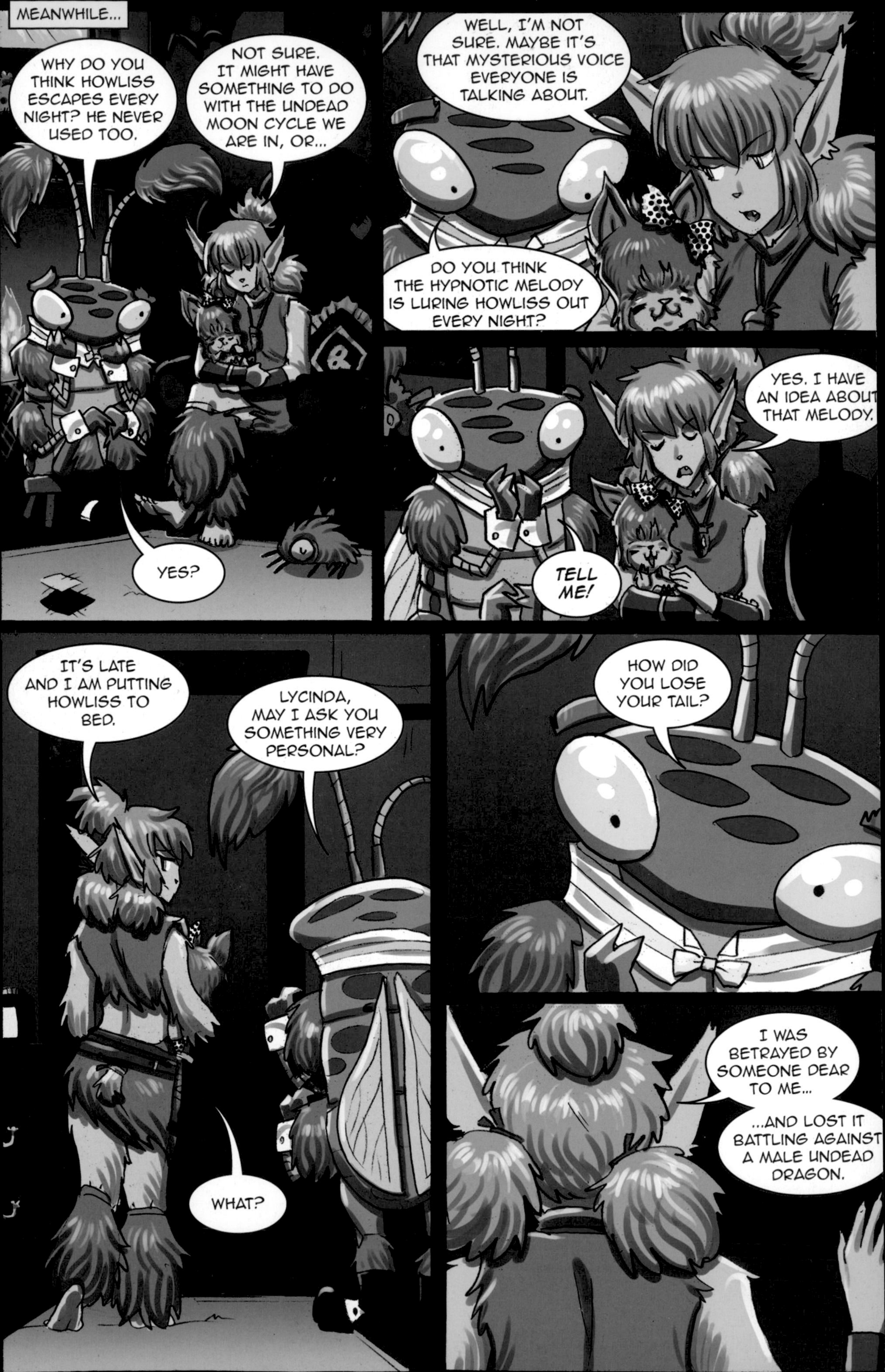
MEANWHILE...
WHY DO YOU THINK HOWLISS ESCAPES EVERY NIGHT? HE NEVER USED TOO.
NOT SURE. IT MIGHT HAVE SOMETHING TO DO WITH THE UNDEAD MOON CYCLE WE ARE IN, OR...
YES?
WELL, I'M NOT SURE. MAYBE IT'S THAT MYSTERIOUS VOICE EVERYONE IS TALKING ABOUT.
DO YOU THINK THE HYPNOTIC MELODY IS LURING HOWLISS OUT EVERY NIGHT?
YES. I HAVE AN IDEA ABOUT THAT MELODY.
TELL ME!
IT'S LATE AND I AM PUTTING HOWLISS TO BED.
LYCINDA, MAY I ASK YOU SOMETHING VERY PERSONAL?
WHAT?
HOW DID YOU LOSE YOUR TAIL?
I WAS BETRAYED BY SOMEONE DEAR TO ME...
...AND LOST IT BATTLING AGAINST A MALE UNDEAD DRAGON.

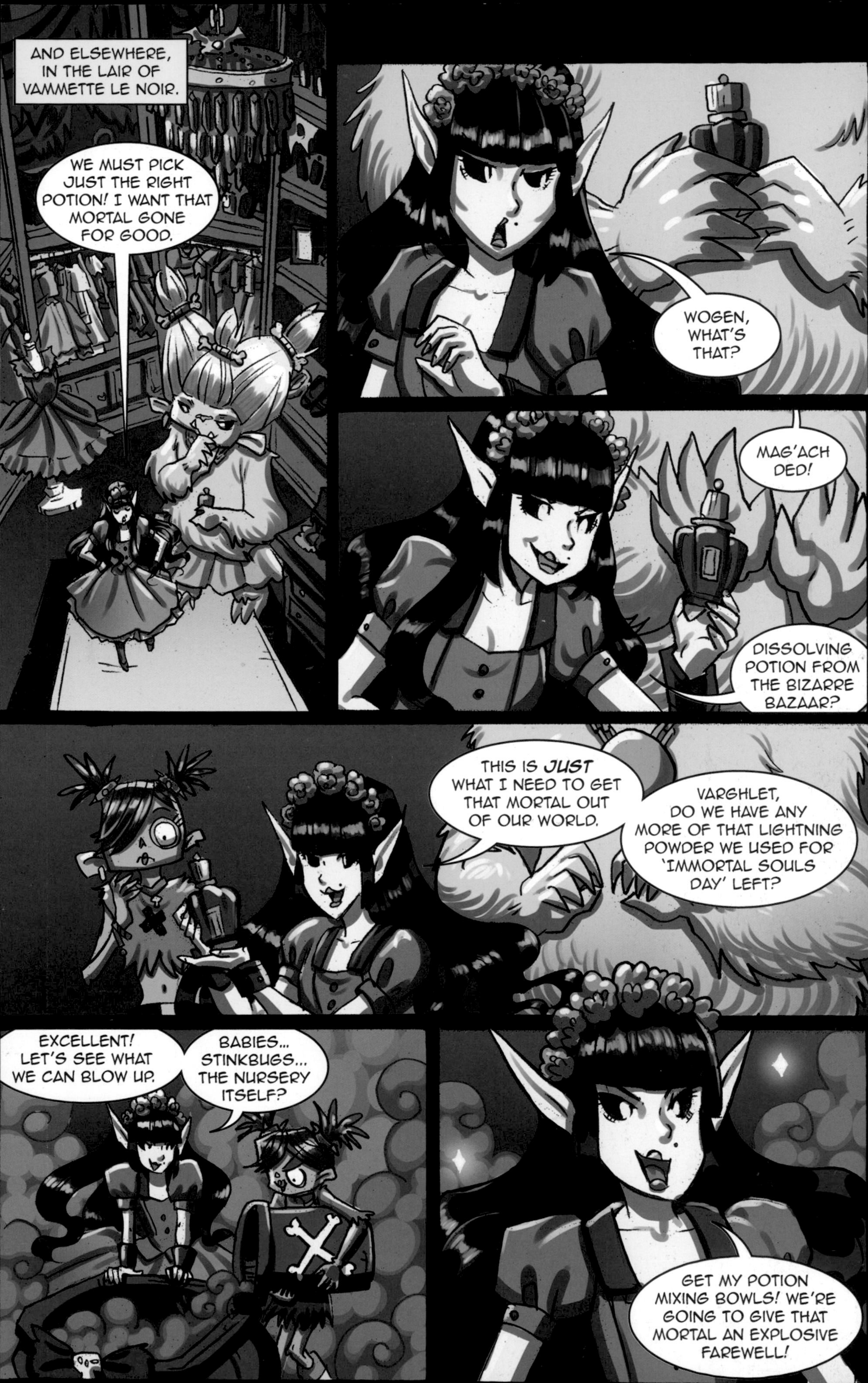
AND ELSEWHERE, IN THE LAIR OF VAMMETTE LE NOIR.
WE MUST PICK JUST THE RIGHT POTION! I WANT THAT MORTAL GONE FOR GOOD.
WOGEN, WHAT'S THAT?
MAG'ACH DED!
DISSOLVING POTION FROM THE BIZARRE BAZAAR?
THIS IS JUST WHAT I NEED TO GET THAT MORTAL OUT OF OUR WORLD.
VARGHLET, DO WE HAVE ANY MORE OF THAT LIGHTNING POWDER WE USED FOR 'IMMORTAL SOULS DAY' LEFT?
EXCELLENT! LET'S SEE WHAT WE CAN BLOW UP.
BABIES... STINKBUGS... THE NURSERY ITSELF?
GET MY POTION MIXING BOWLS! WE'RE GOING TO GIVE THAT MORTAL AN EXPLOSIVE FAREWELL!

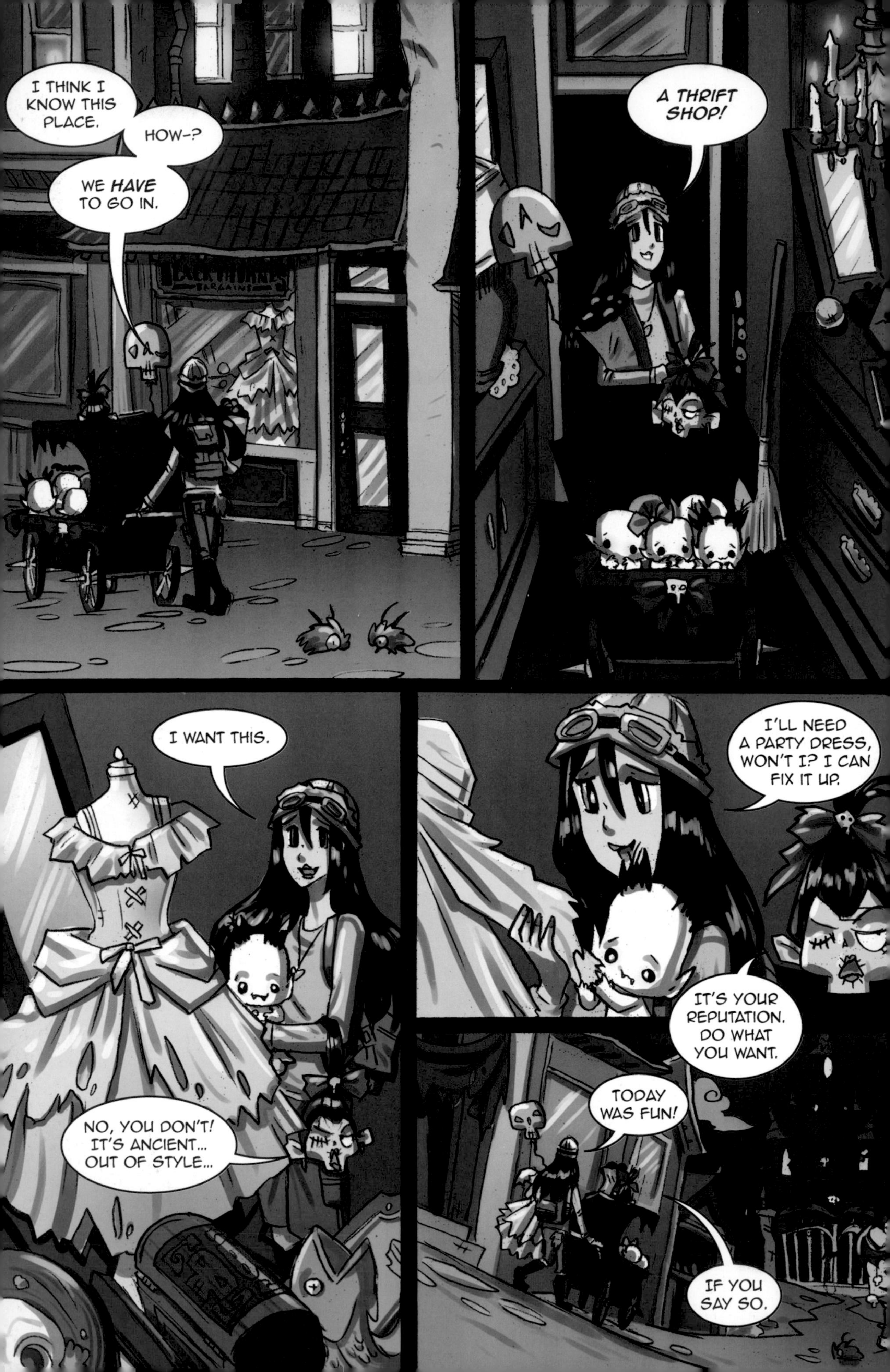

I THINK I KNOW THIS PLACE.
HOW-?
WE *HAVE* TO GO IN.
BLACKTHORNE BARGAINS
*A THRIFT SHOP!*
I WANT THIS.
NO, YOU DON'T! IT'S ANCIENT... OUT OF STYLE...
I'LL NEED A PARTY DRESS, WON'T I? I CAN FIX IT UP.
IT'S YOUR REPUTATION. DO WHAT YOU WANT.
TODAY WAS FUN!
IF YOU SAY SO.

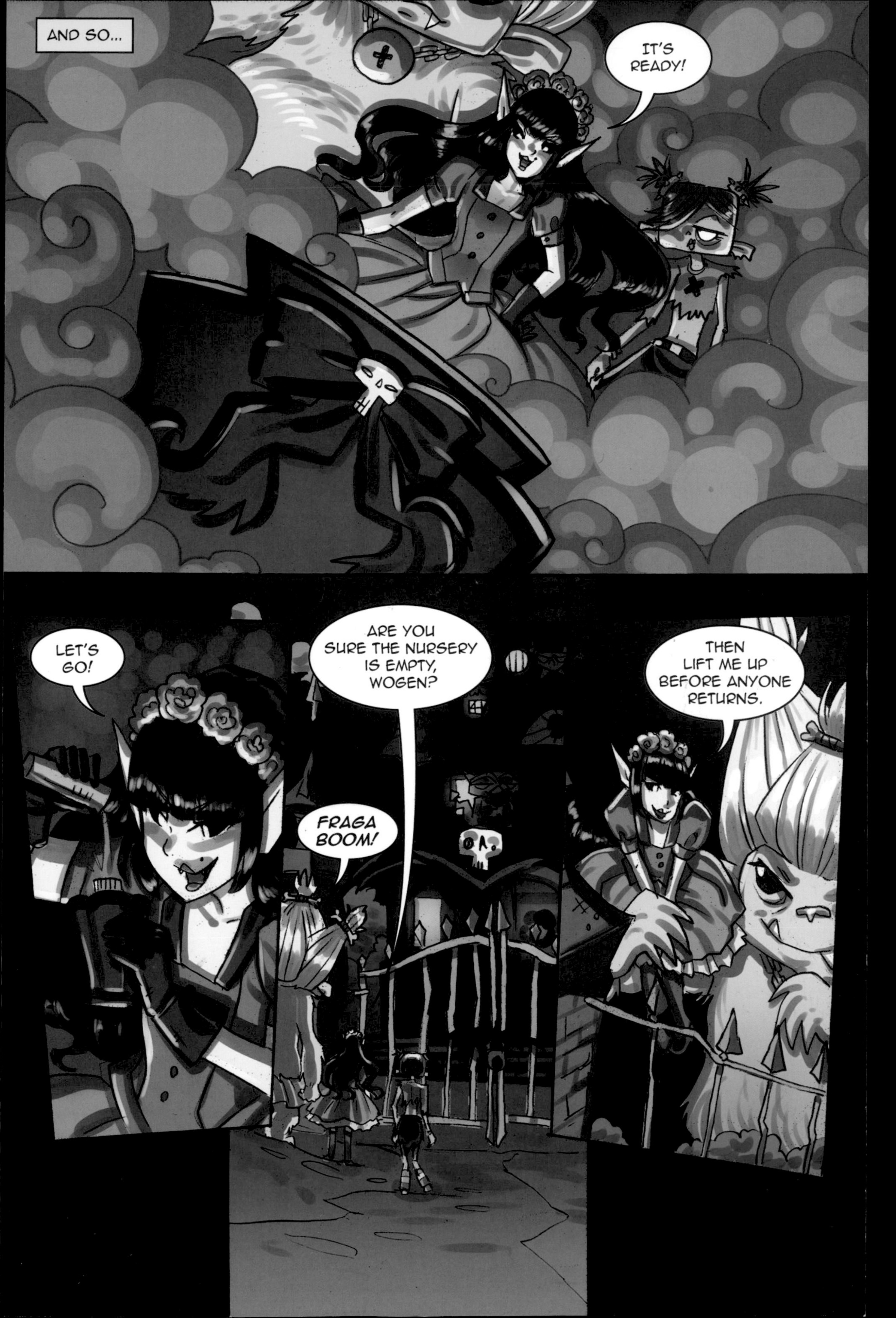
AND SO...
IT'S READY!
LET'S GO!
ARE YOU SURE THE NURSERY IS EMPTY, WOGEN?
FRAGA BOOM!
THEN LIFT ME UP BEFORE ANYONE RETURNS.

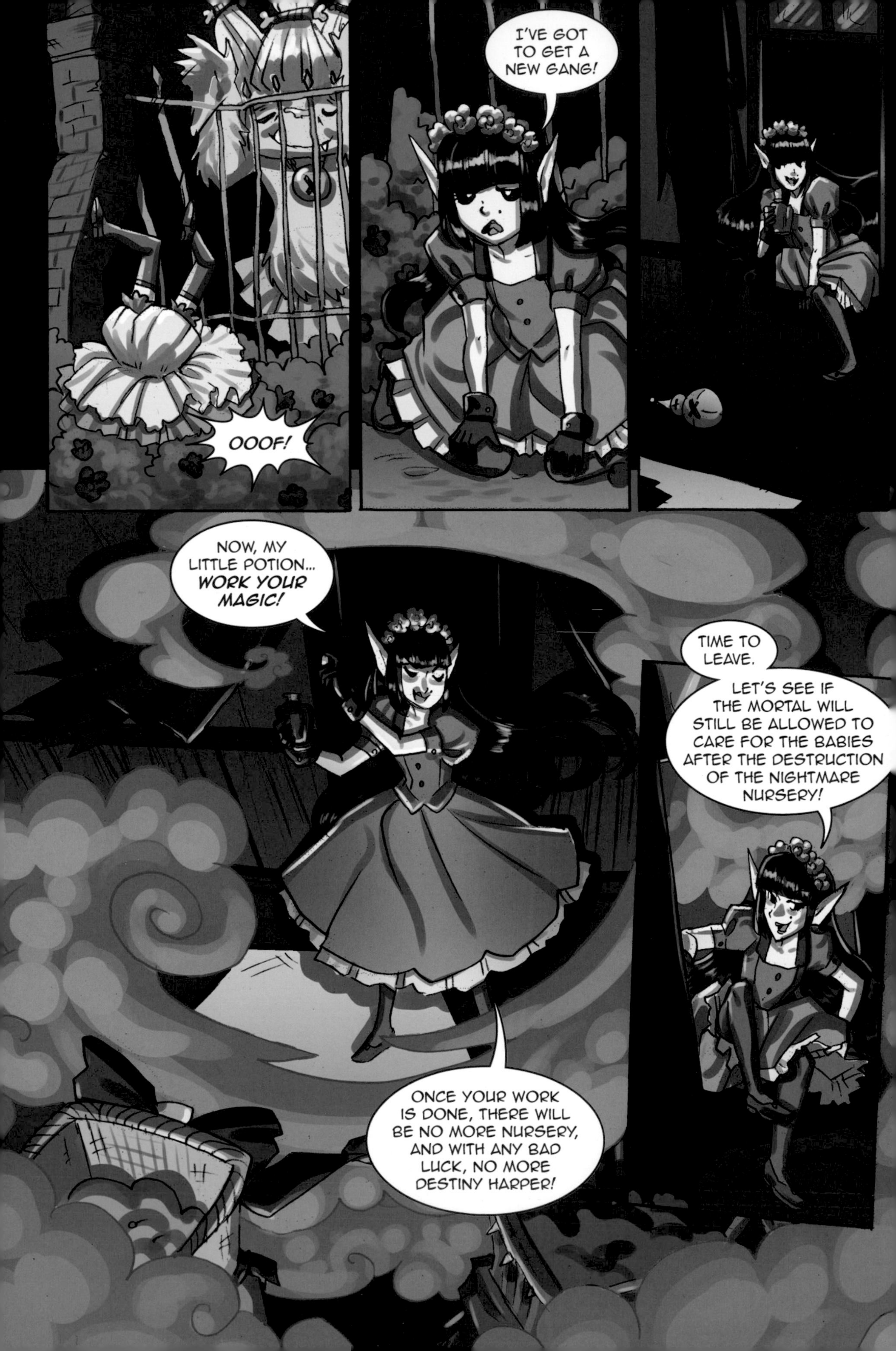
OOOF!
I'VE GOT TO GET A NEW GANG!
NOW, MY LITTLE POTION... WORK YOUR MAGIC!
ONCE YOUR WORK IS DONE, THERE WILL BE NO MORE NURSERY, AND WITH ANY BAD LUCK, NO MORE DESTINY HARPER!
TIME TO LEAVE.
LET'S SEE IF THE MORTAL WILL STILL BE ALLOWED TO CARE FOR THE BABIES AFTER THE DESTRUCTION OF THE NIGHTMARE NURSERY!

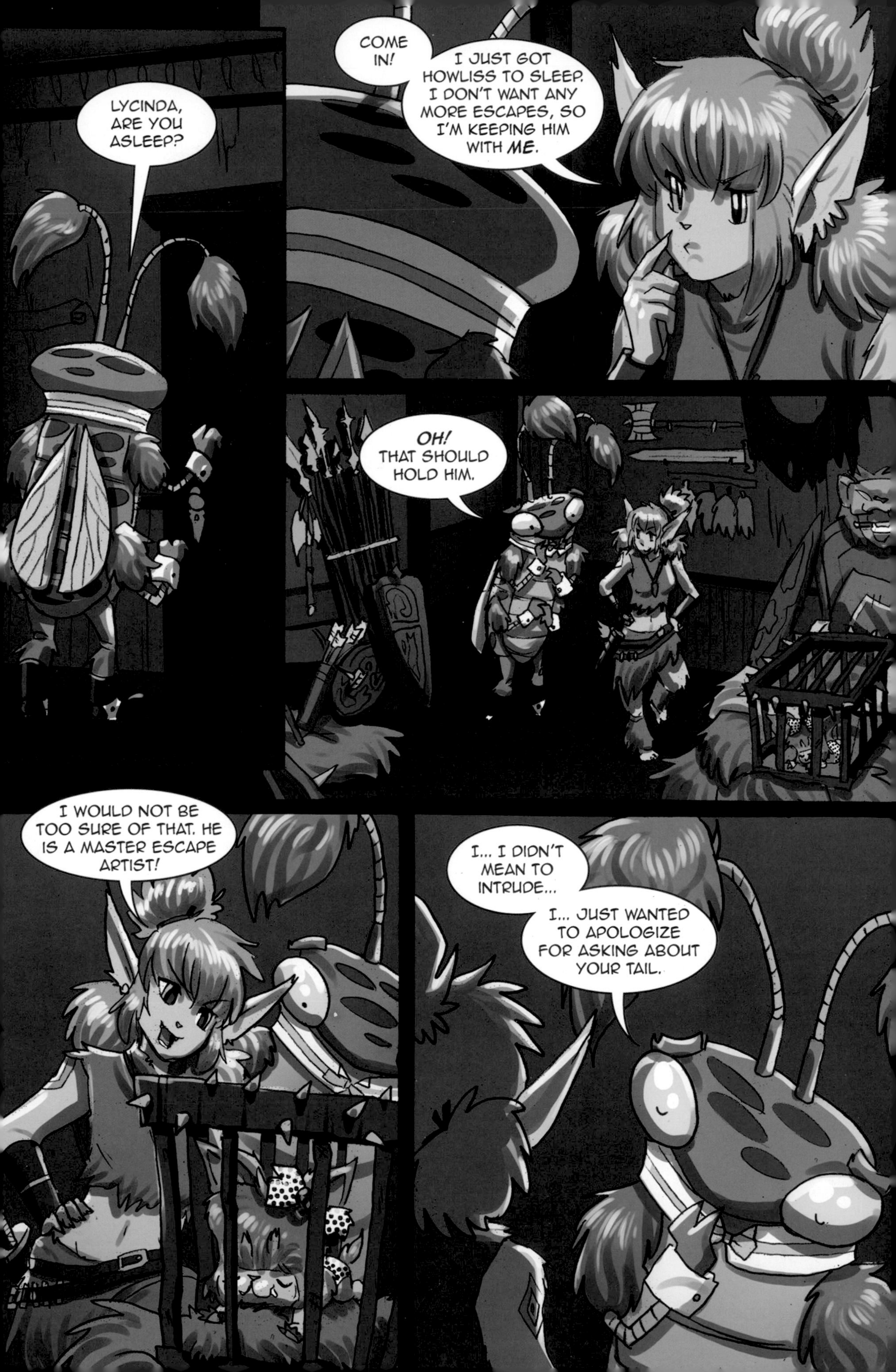
LYCINDA, ARE YOU ASLEEP?
COME IN!
I JUST GOT HOWLISS TO SLEEP. I DON'T WANT ANY MORE ESCAPES, SO I'M KEEPING HIM WITH ME.
OH! THAT SHOULD HOLD HIM.
I WOULD NOT BE TOO SURE OF THAT. HE IS A MASTER ESCAPE ARTIST!
I... I DIDN'T MEAN TO INTRUDE...
I... JUST WANTED TO APOLOGIZE FOR ASKING ABOUT YOUR TAIL.

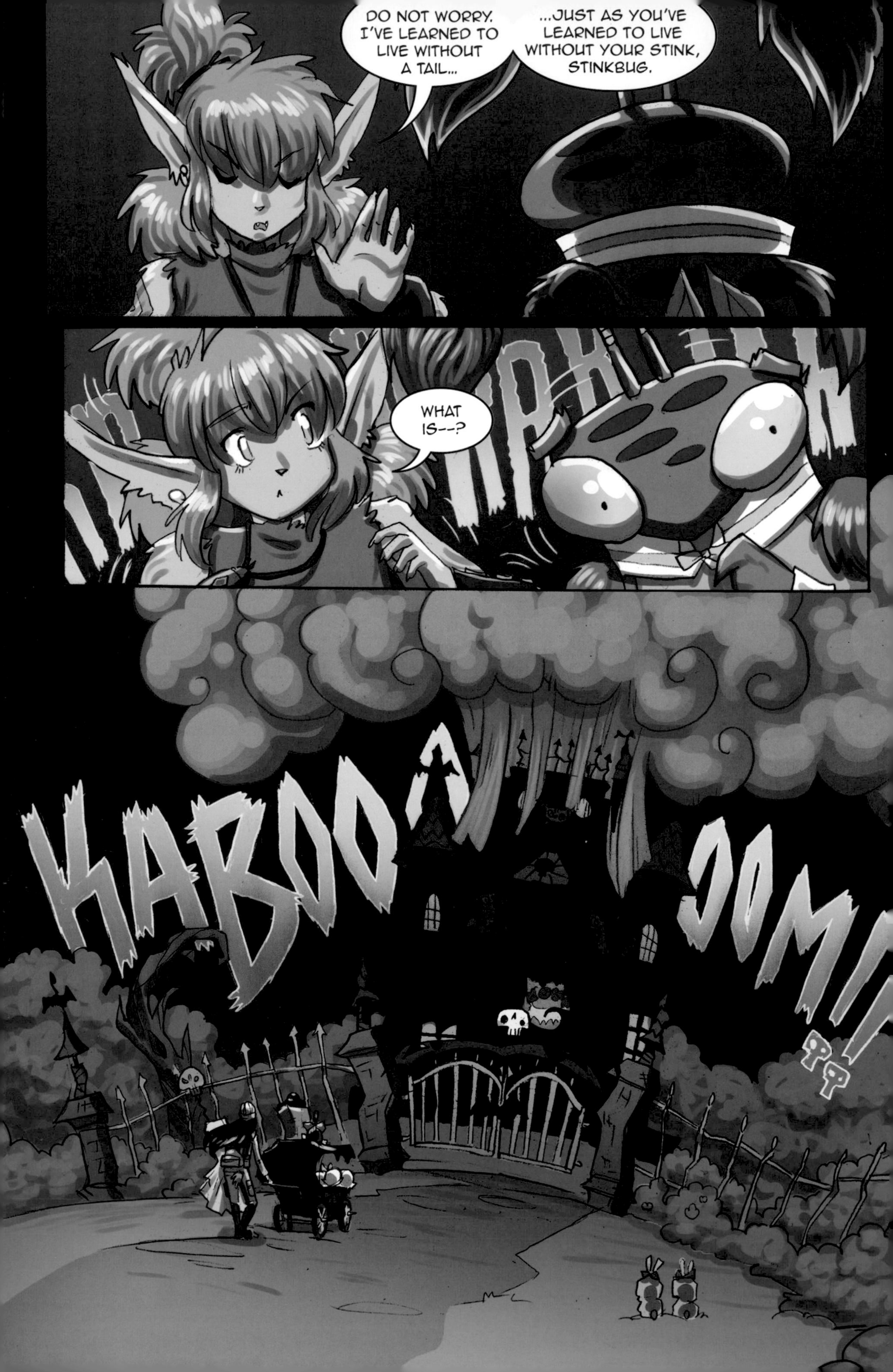
DO NOT WORRY. I'VE LEARNED TO LIVE WITHOUT A TAIL...
...JUST AS YOU'VE LEARNED TO LIVE WITHOUT YOUR STINK, STINKBUG.
WHAT IS--?
KABOOOOM!!

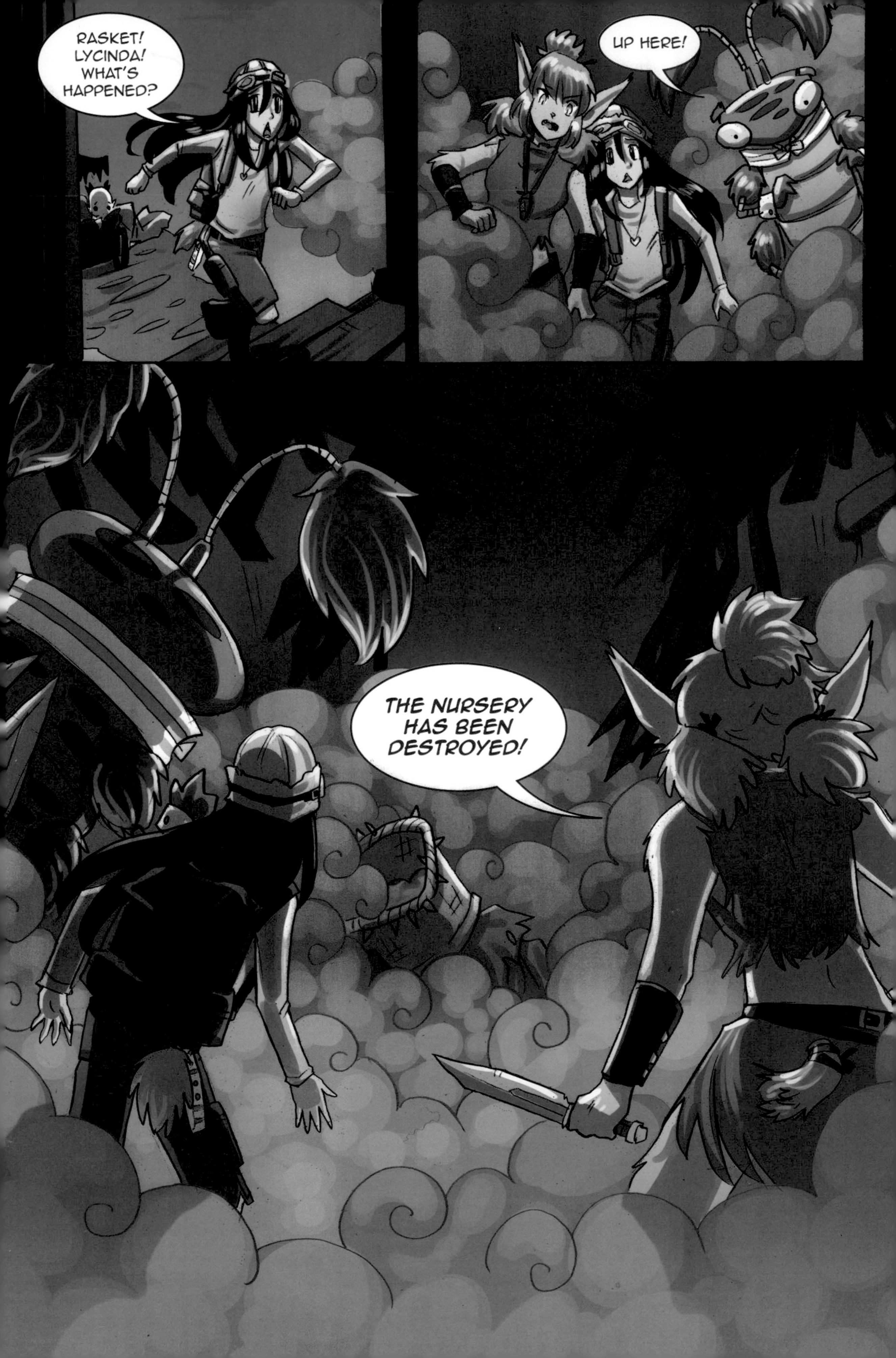
RASKET! LYCINDA! WHAT'S HAPPENED?
UP HERE!
THE NURSERY HAS BEEN DESTROYED!

# CHAPTER 6

## "DANCE OF THE POISON BLACK MUSHROOM FAIRIES"

WRITTEN BY GAYLE MIDDLETON AND DAVE DWONCH
DRAWN BY AMANDA CORONADO
COLOR ART BY BILL BLANKENSHIP
LETTERED BY DAVE DWONCH

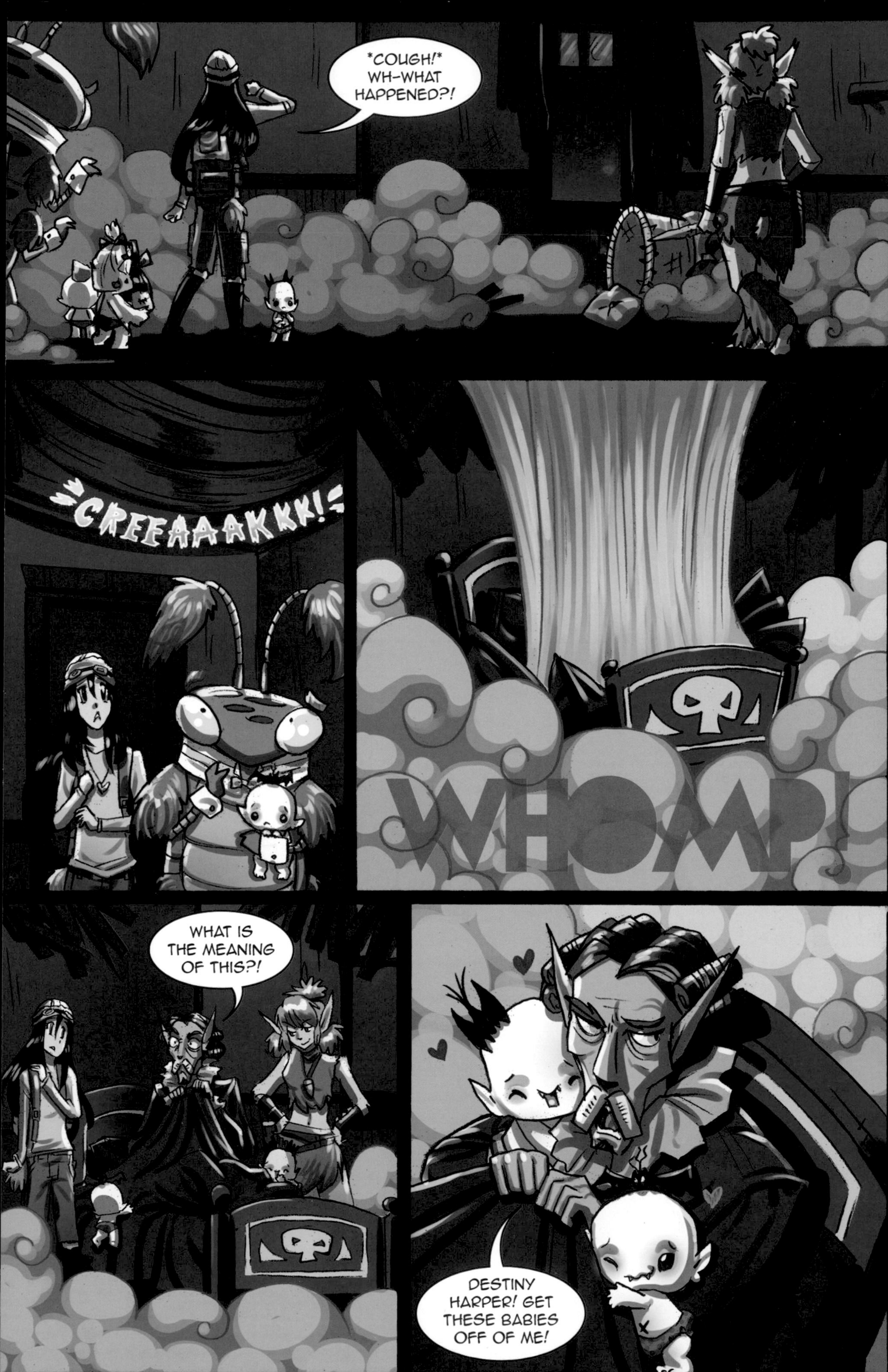
*COUGH!* WH-WHAT HAPPENED?!
CREEAAAKKK!
WHOMP!
WHAT IS THE MEANING OF THIS?!
DESTINY HARPER! GET THESE BABIES OFF OF ME!

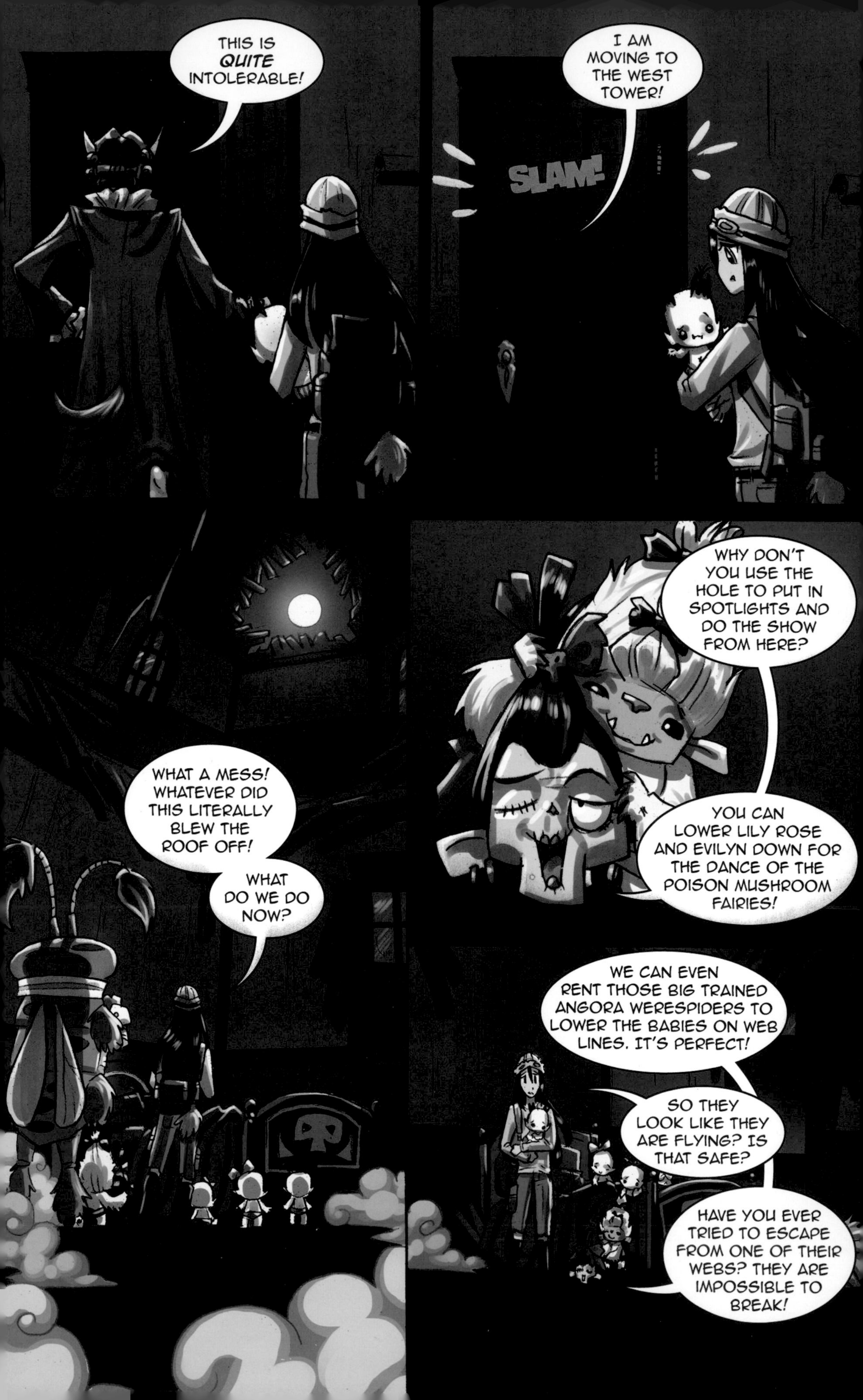
THIS IS QUITE INTOLERABLE!
I AM MOVING TO THE WEST TOWER!
SLAM!
WHAT A MESS! WHATEVER DID THIS LITERALLY BLEW THE ROOF OFF!
WHAT DO WE DO NOW?
WHY DON'T YOU USE THE HOLE TO PUT IN SPOTLIGHTS AND DO THE SHOW FROM HERE?
YOU CAN LOWER LILY ROSE AND EVILYN DOWN FOR THE DANCE OF THE POISON MUSHROOM FAIRIES!
WE CAN EVEN RENT THOSE BIG TRAINED ANGORA WERESPIDERS TO LOWER THE BABIES ON WEB LINES. IT'S PERFECT!
SO THEY LOOK LIKE THEY ARE FLYING? IS THAT SAFE?
HAVE YOU EVER TRIED TO ESCAPE FROM ONE OF THEIR WEBS? THEY ARE IMPOSSIBLE TO BREAK!

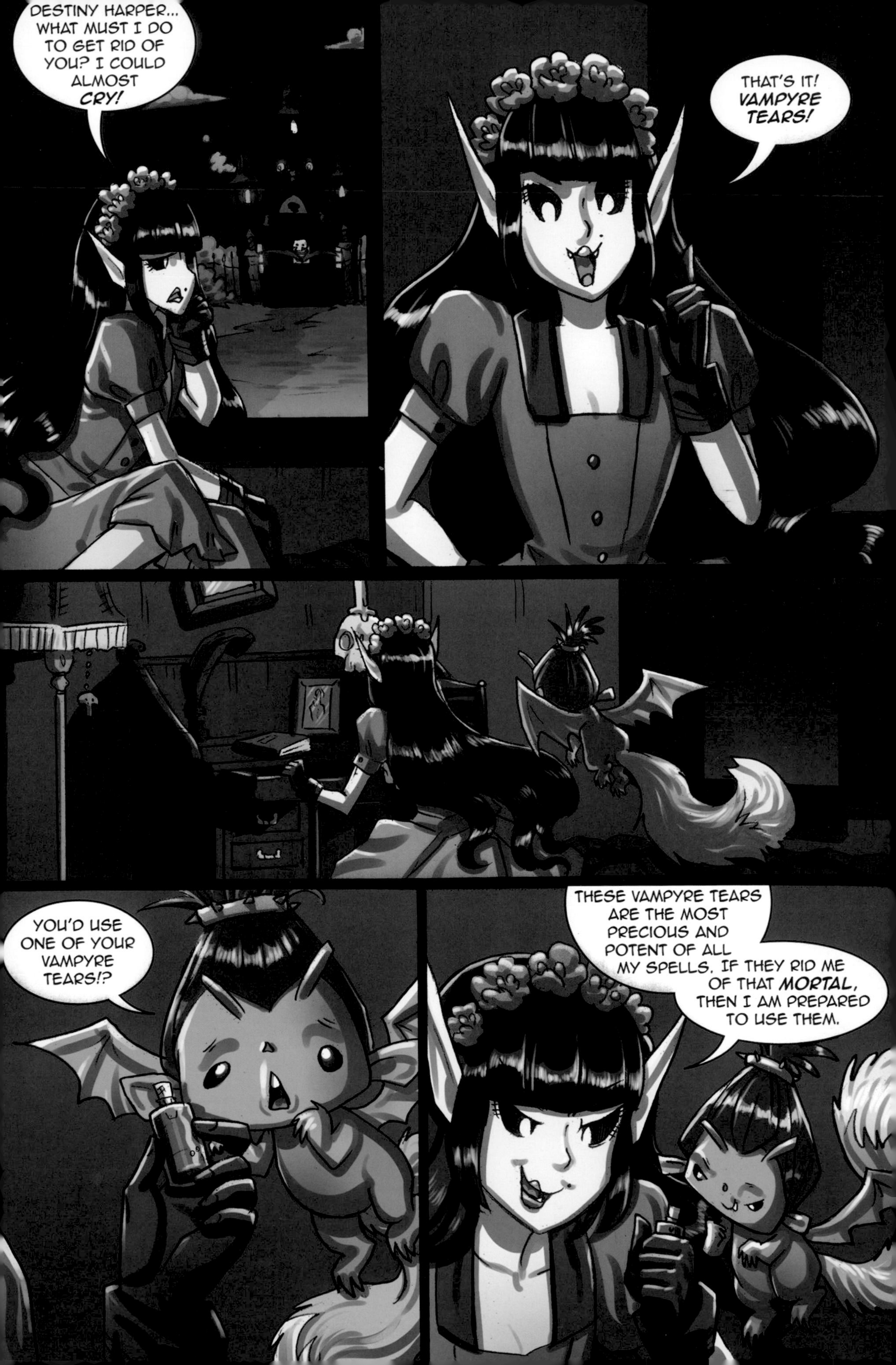
DESTINY HARPER... WHAT MUST I DO TO GET RID OF YOU? I COULD ALMOST *CRY!*
THAT'S IT! *VAMPYRE TEARS!*
YOU'D USE ONE OF YOUR VAMPYRE TEARS!?
THESE VAMPYRE TEARS ARE THE MOST PRECIOUS AND POTENT OF ALL MY SPELLS. IF THEY RID ME OF THAT *MORTAL*, THEN I AM PREPARED TO USE THEM.

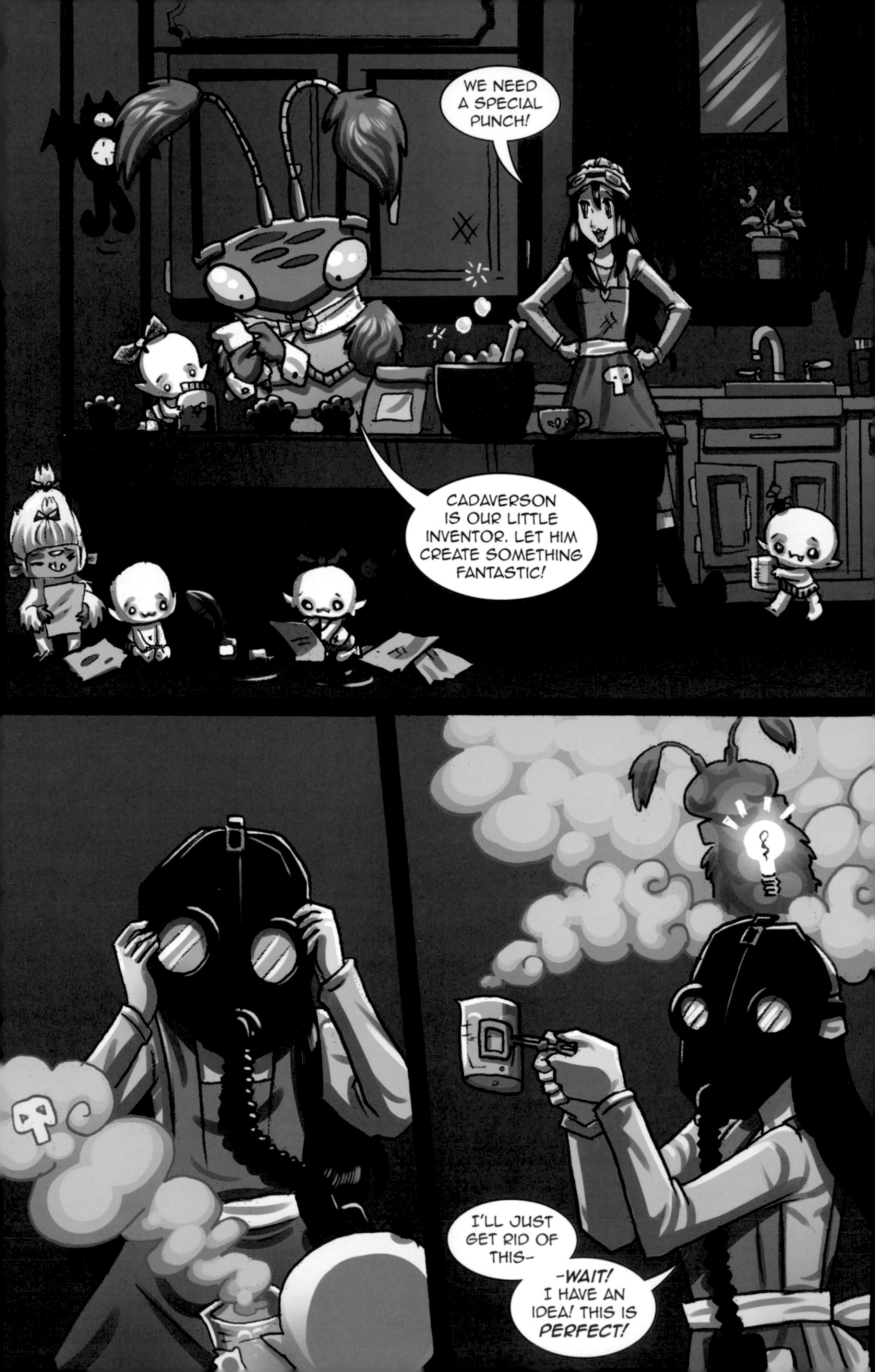
WE NEED A SPECIAL PUNCH!
CADAVERSON IS OUR LITTLE INVENTOR. LET HIM CREATE SOMETHING FANTASTIC!
I'LL JUST GET RID OF THIS-
-WAIT! I HAVE AN IDEA! THIS IS PERFECT!

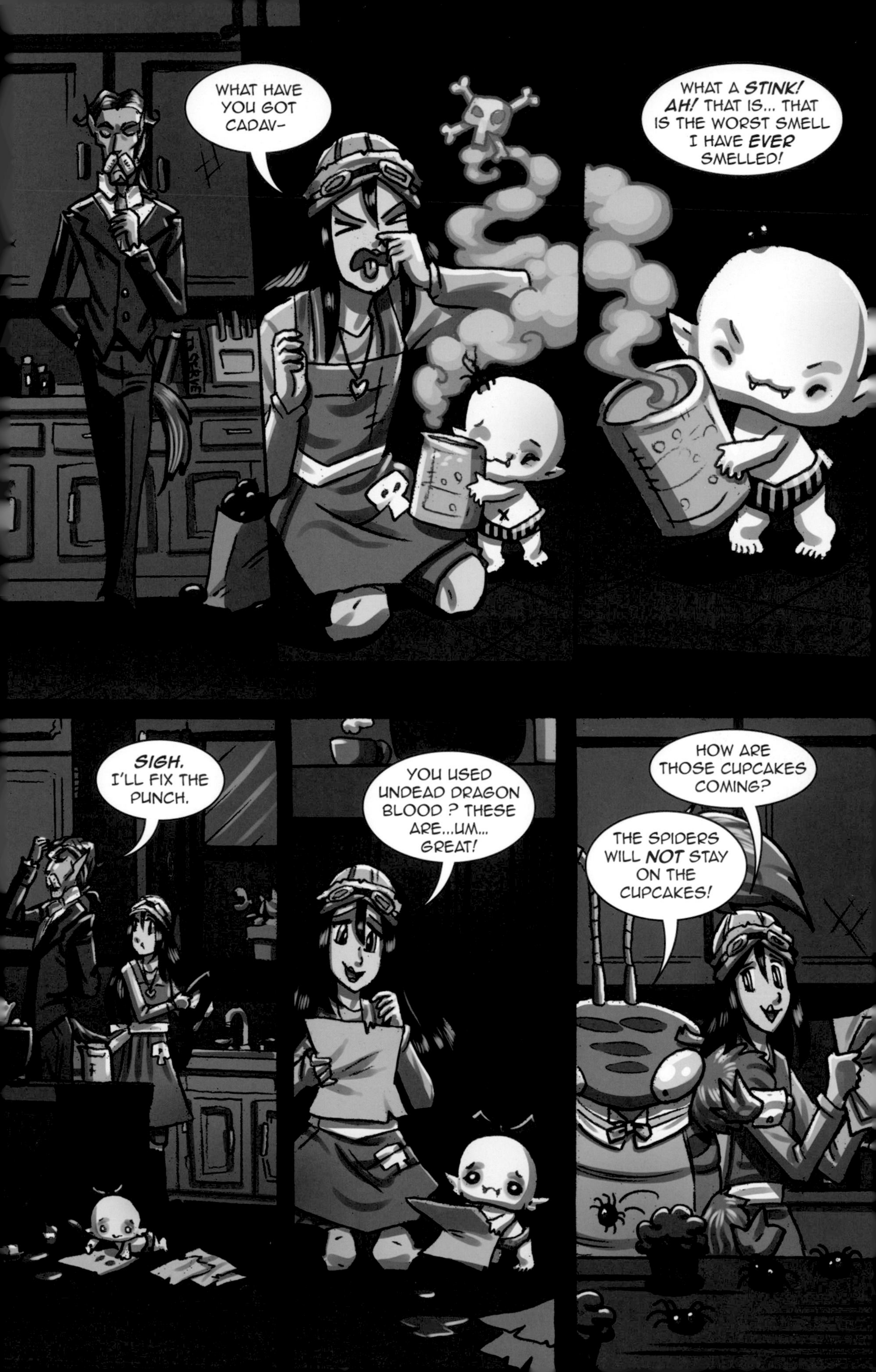
WHAT HAVE YOU GOT CADAV-
WHAT A STINK! AH! THAT IS... THAT IS THE WORST SMELL I HAVE EVER SMELLED!
SIGH. I'LL FIX THE PUNCH.
YOU USED UNDEAD DRAGON BLOOD ? THESE ARE...UM... GREAT!
HOW ARE THOSE CUPCAKES COMING?
THE SPIDERS WILL NOT STAY ON THE CUPCAKES!

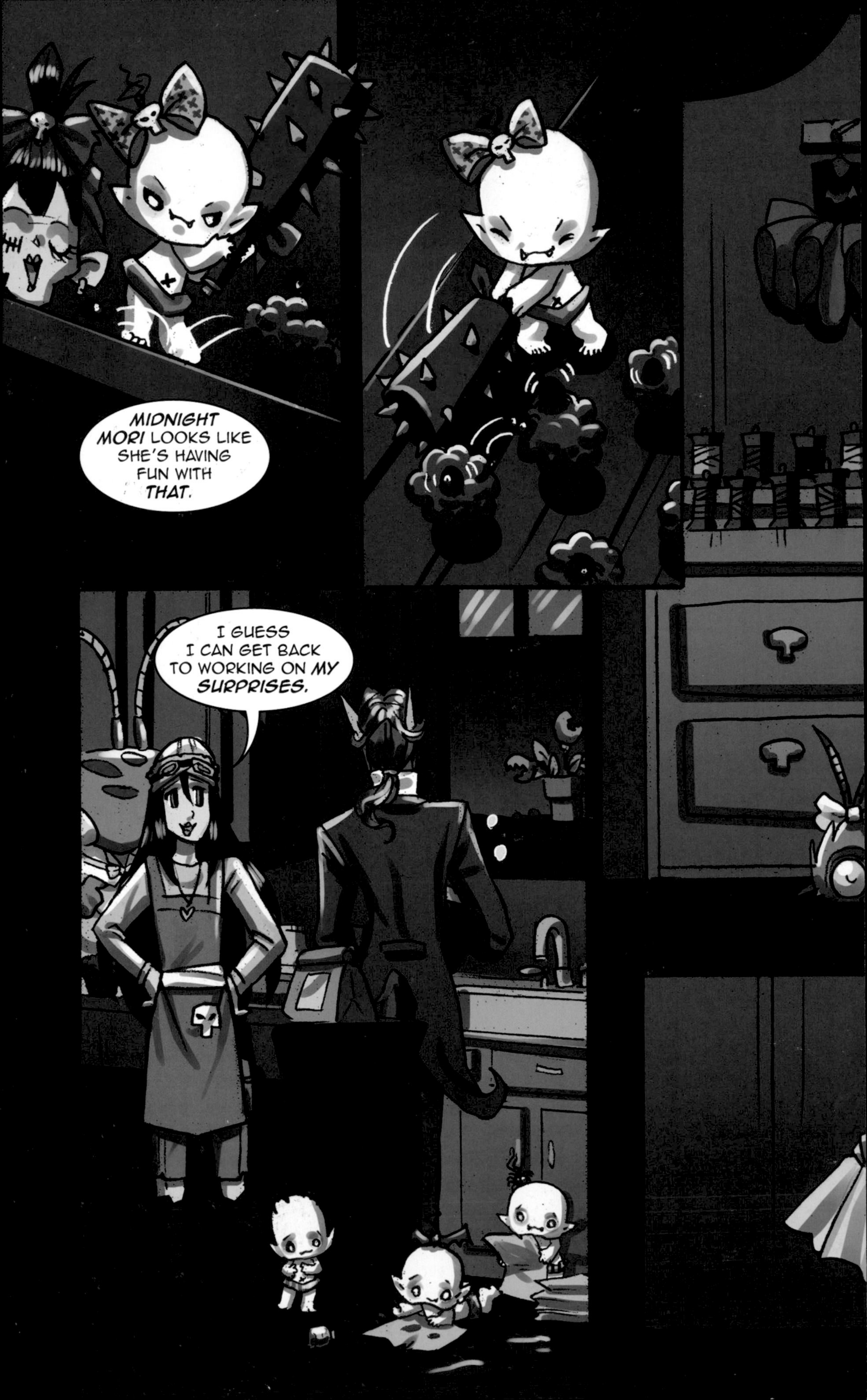
MIDNIGHT MORI LOOKS LIKE SHE'S HAVING FUN WITH THAT.
I GUESS I CAN GET BACK TO WORKING ON MY SURPRISES.

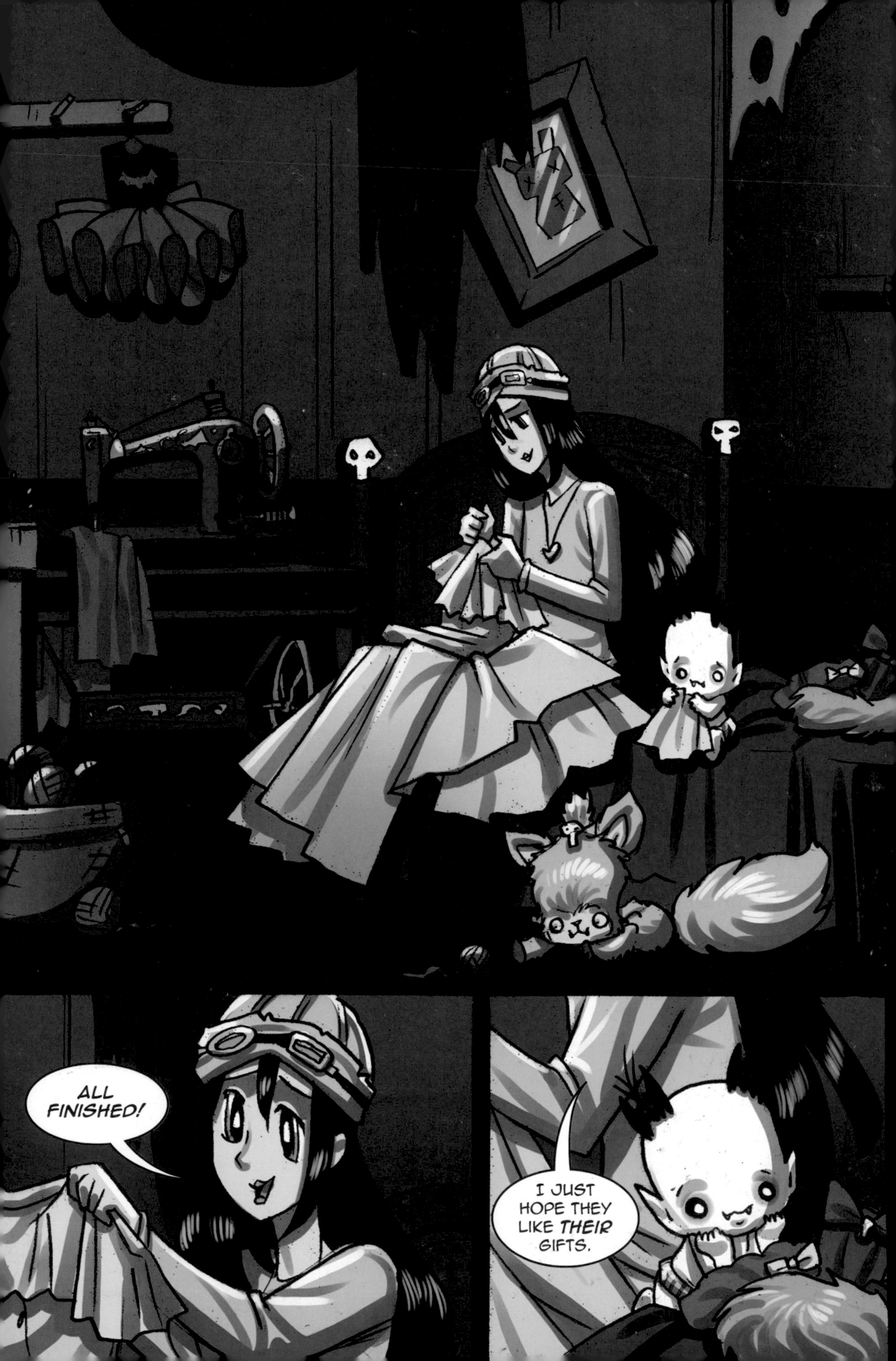
ALL FINISHED!
I JUST HOPE THEY LIKE *THEIR* GIFTS.

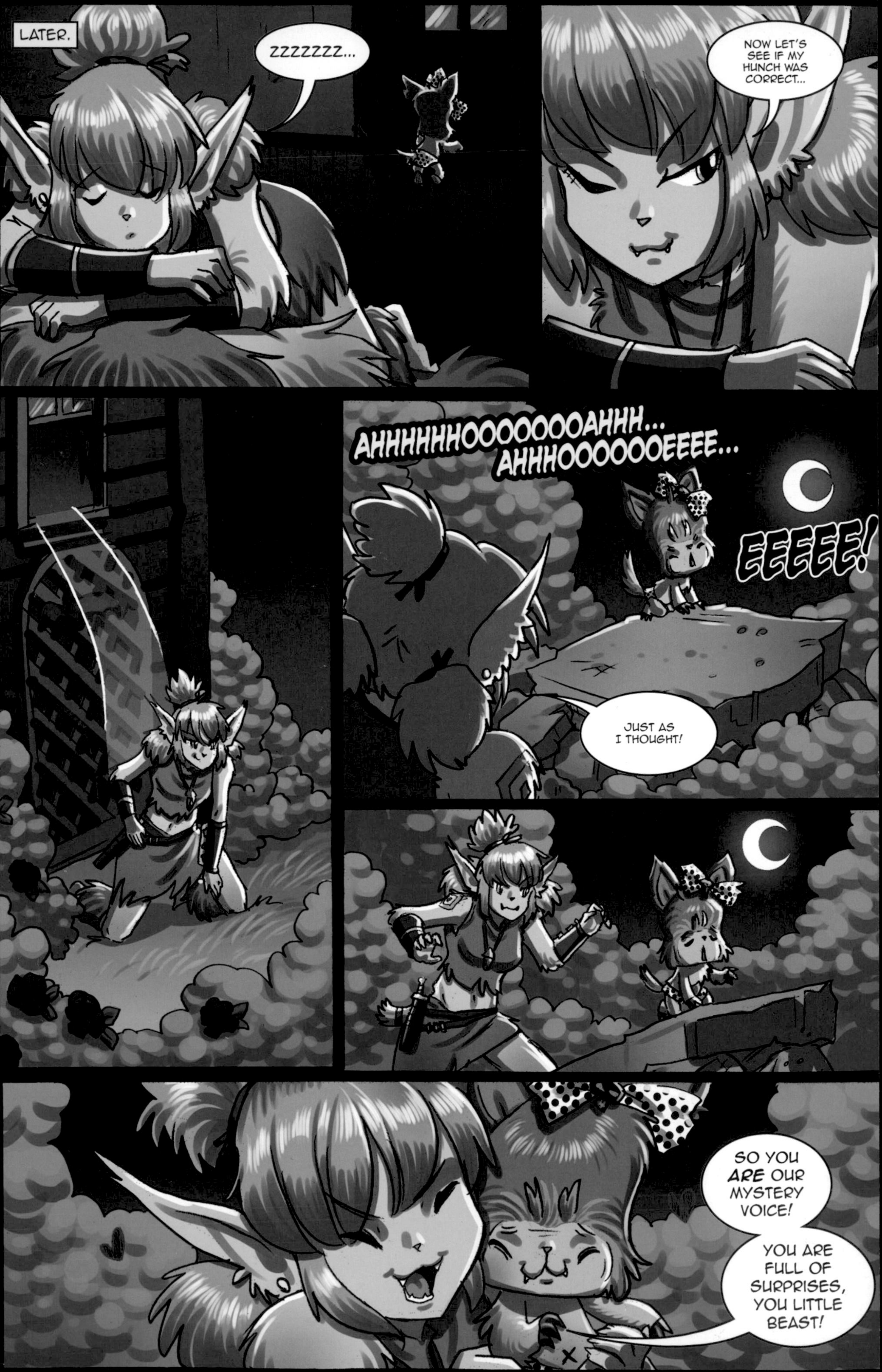

LATER.
ZZZZZZZ...
NOW LET'S SEE IF MY HUNCH WAS CORRECT...
AHHHHHHOOOOOOOAHHH... AHHHOOOOOOEEEE...
EEEEE!
JUST AS I THOUGHT!
SO YOU ARE OUR MYSTERY VOICE!
YOU ARE FULL OF SURPRISES, YOU LITTLE BEAST!

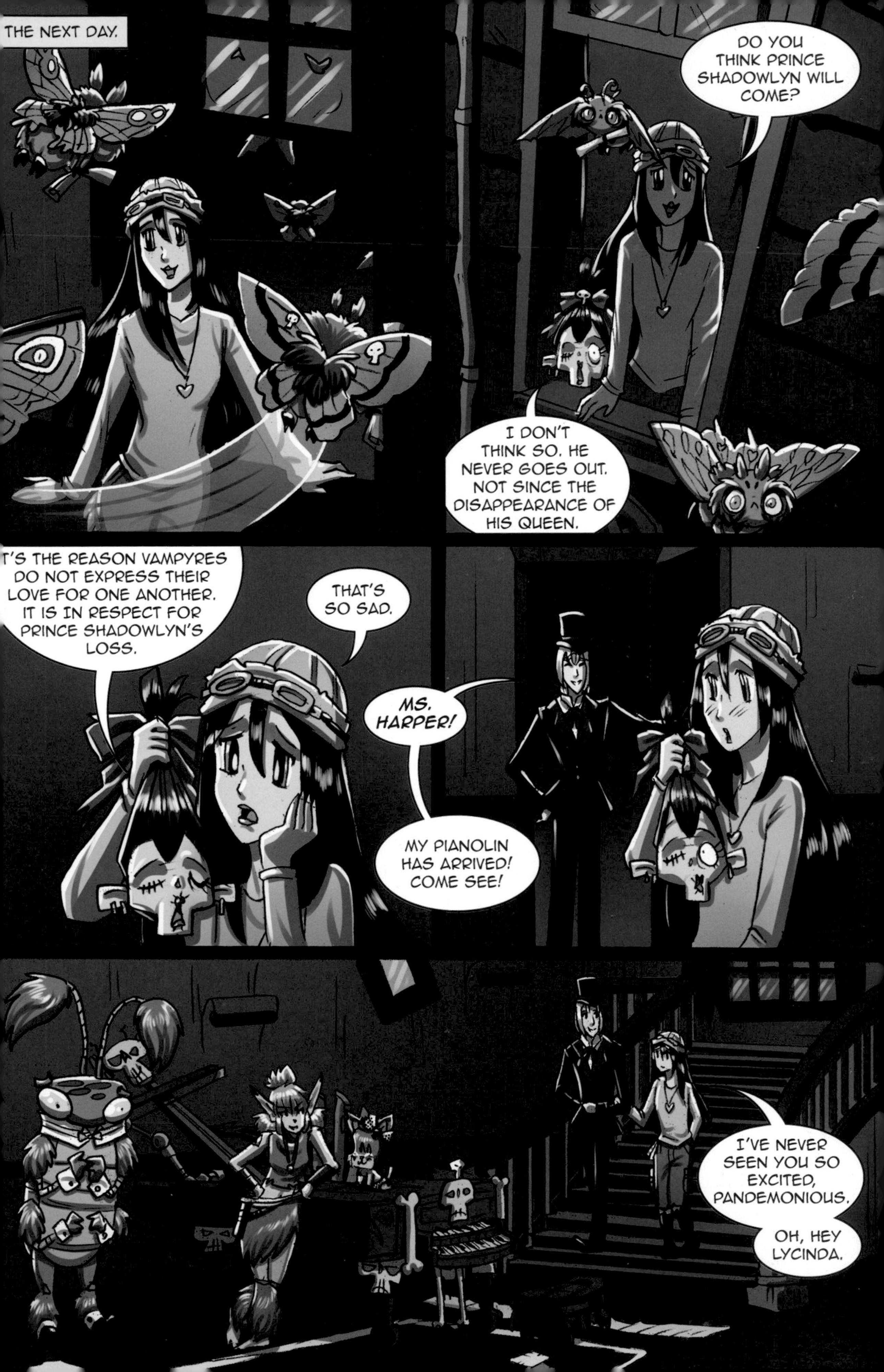
THE NEXT DAY.
DO YOU THINK PRINCE SHADOWLYN WILL COME?
I DON'T THINK SO. HE NEVER GOES OUT. NOT SINCE THE DISAPPEARANCE OF HIS QUEEN.
IT'S THE REASON VAMPYRES DO NOT EXPRESS THEIR LOVE FOR ONE ANOTHER. IT IS IN RESPECT FOR PRINCE SHADOWLYN'S LOSS.
THAT'S SO SAD.
MS. HARPER!
MY PIANOLIN HAS ARRIVED! COME SEE!
I'VE NEVER SEEN YOU SO EXCITED, PANDEMONIOUS.
OH, HEY LYCINDA.

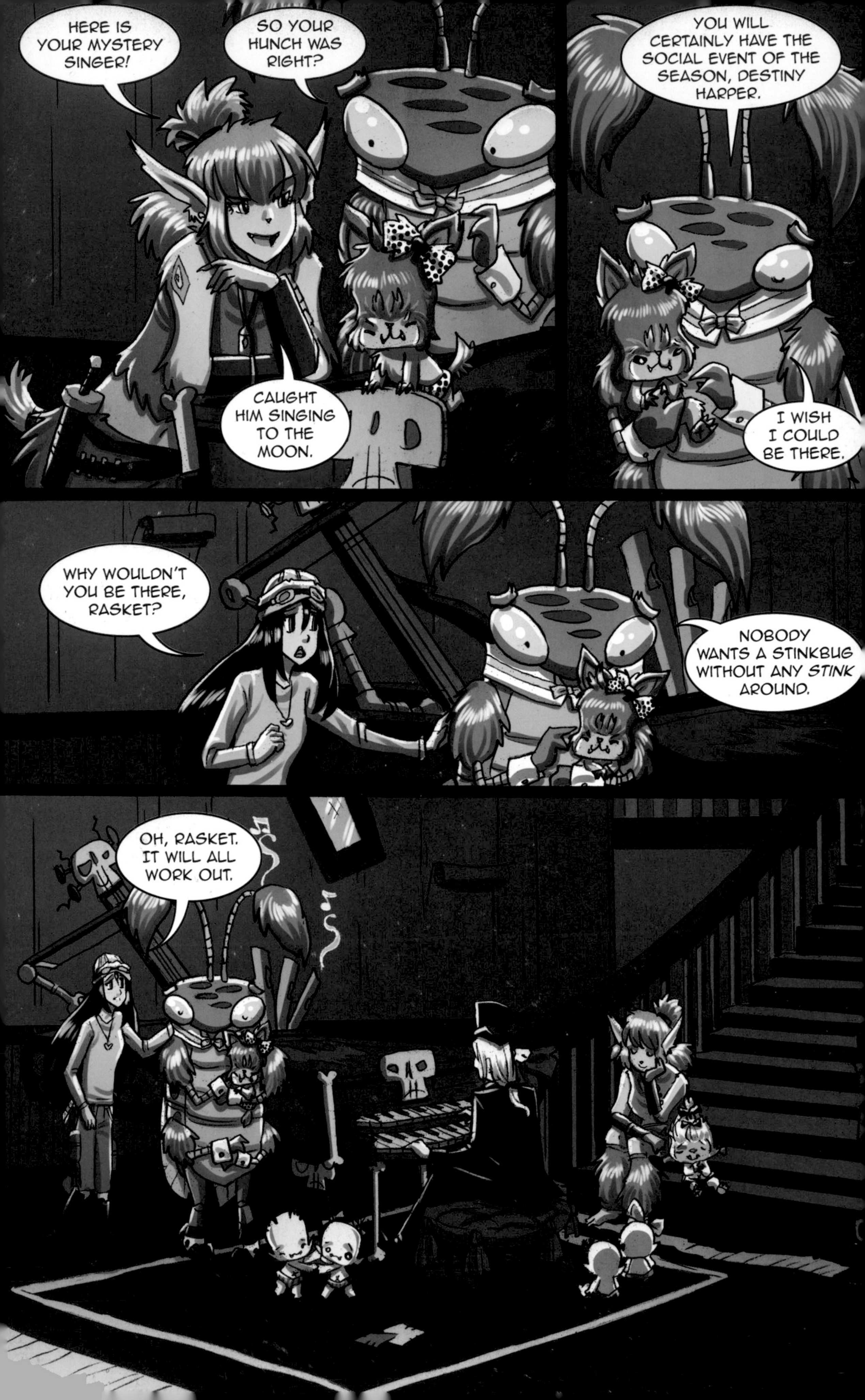
HERE IS YOUR MYSTERY SINGER!
SO YOUR HUNCH WAS RIGHT?
CAUGHT HIM SINGING TO THE MOON.
YOU WILL CERTAINLY HAVE THE SOCIAL EVENT OF THE SEASON, DESTINY HARPER.
I WISH I COULD BE THERE.
WHY WOULDN'T YOU BE THERE, RASKET?
NOBODY WANTS A STINKBUG WITHOUT ANY *STINK* AROUND.
OH, RASKET. IT WILL ALL WORK OUT.

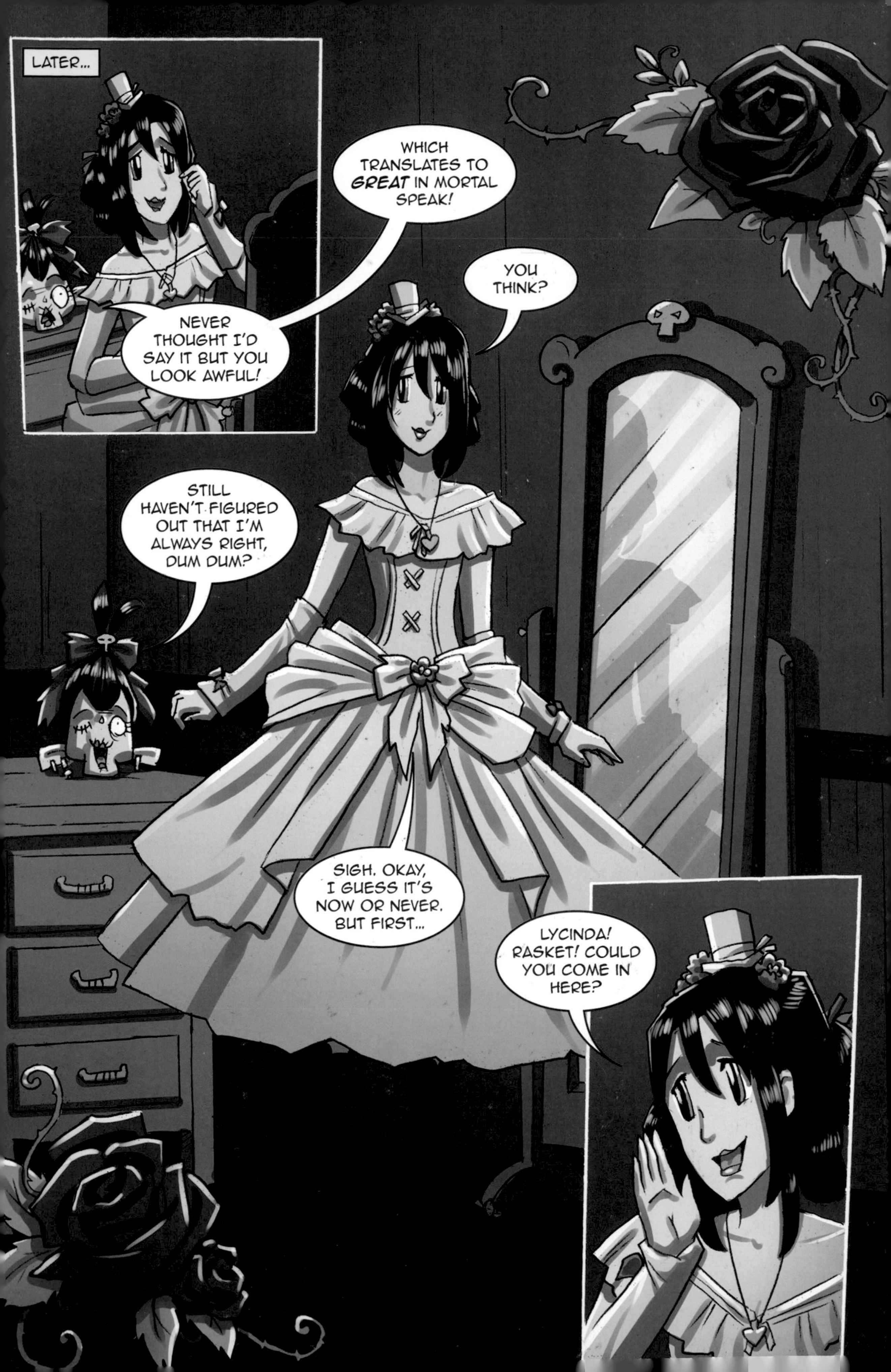
LATER...
NEVER THOUGHT I'D SAY IT BUT YOU LOOK AWFUL!
WHICH TRANSLATES TO GREAT IN MORTAL SPEAK!
YOU THINK?
STILL HAVEN'T FIGURED OUT THAT I'M ALWAYS RIGHT, DUM DUM?
SIGH. OKAY, I GUESS IT'S NOW OR NEVER. BUT FIRST...
LYCINDA! RASKET! COULD YOU COME IN HERE?

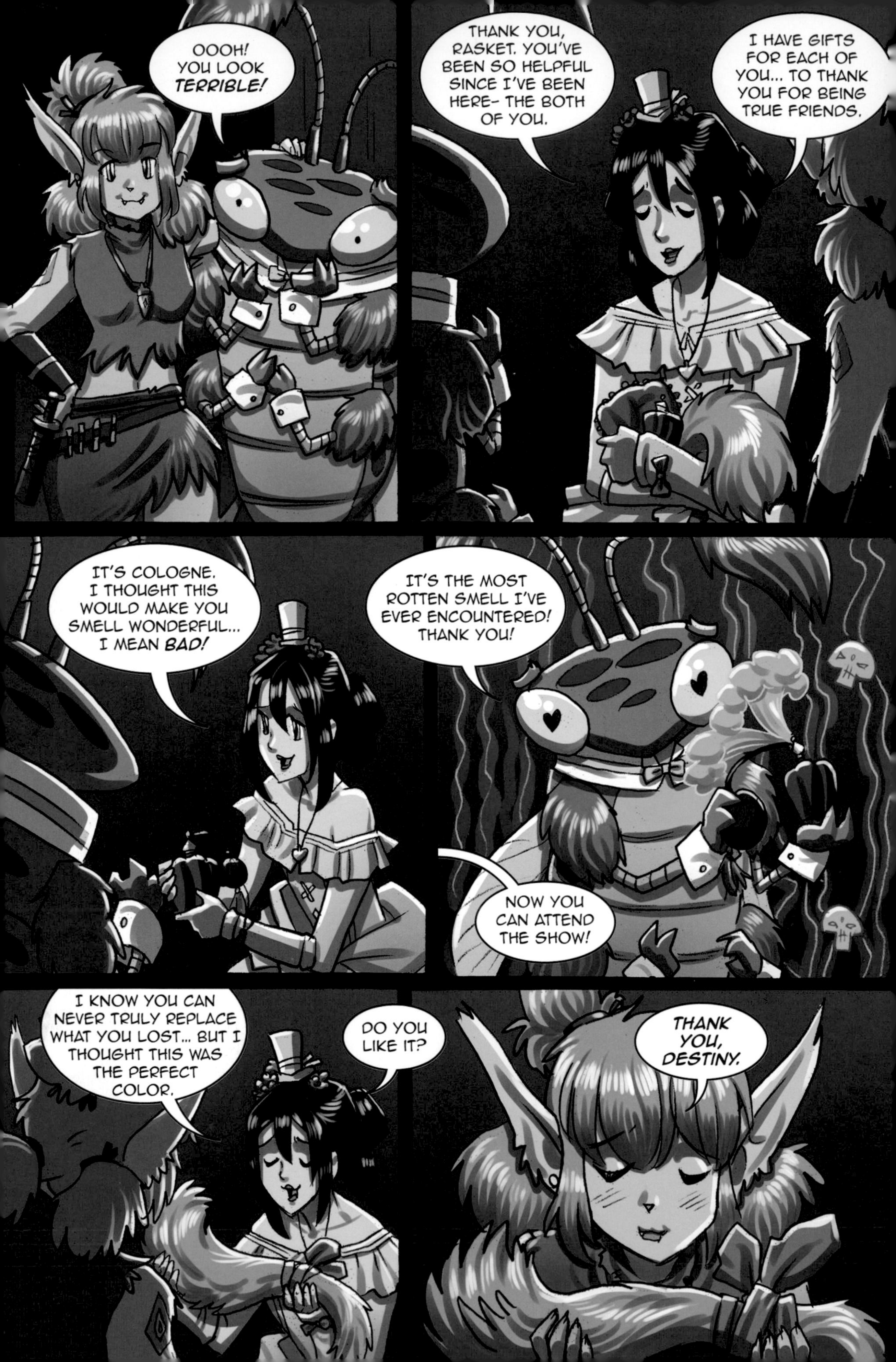
OOOH! YOU LOOK TERRIBLE!
THANK YOU, RASKET. YOU'VE BEEN SO HELPFUL SINCE I'VE BEEN HERE- THE BOTH OF YOU.
I HAVE GIFTS FOR EACH OF YOU... TO THANK YOU FOR BEING TRUE FRIENDS.
IT'S COLOGNE. I THOUGHT THIS WOULD MAKE YOU SMELL WONDERFUL... I MEAN BAD!
IT'S THE MOST ROTTEN SMELL I'VE EVER ENCOUNTERED! THANK YOU!
NOW YOU CAN ATTEND THE SHOW!
I KNOW YOU CAN NEVER TRULY REPLACE WHAT YOU LOST... BUT I THOUGHT THIS WAS THE PERFECT COLOR.
DO YOU LIKE IT?
THANK YOU, DESTINY.

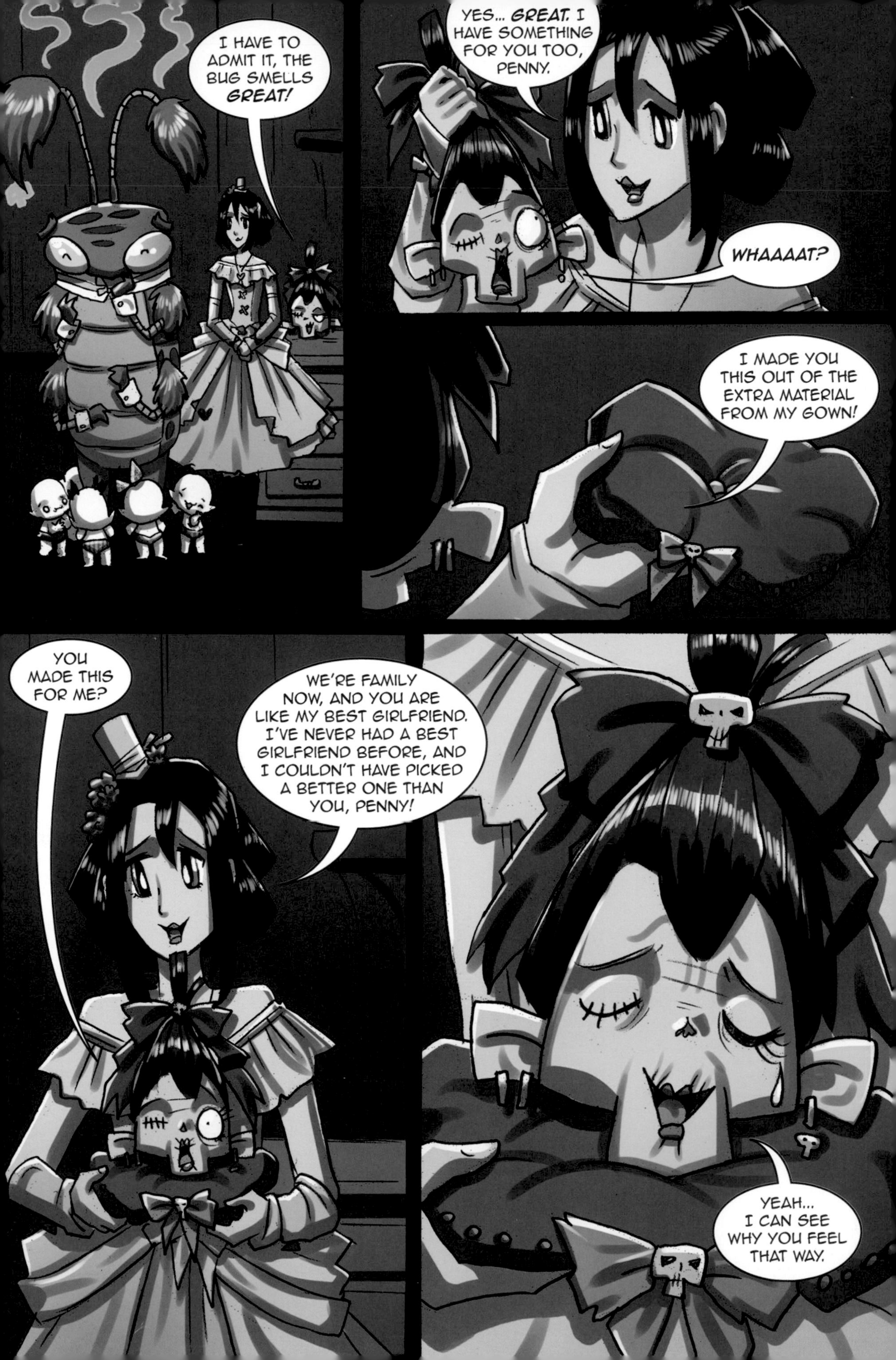
I HAVE TO ADMIT IT, THE BUG SMELLS GREAT!
YES... GREAT. I HAVE SOMETHING FOR YOU TOO, PENNY.
WHAAAAT?
I MADE YOU THIS OUT OF THE EXTRA MATERIAL FROM MY GOWN!
YOU MADE THIS FOR ME?
WE'RE FAMILY NOW, AND YOU ARE LIKE MY BEST GIRLFRIEND. I'VE NEVER HAD A BEST GIRLFRIEND BEFORE, AND I COULDN'T HAVE PICKED A BETTER ONE THAN YOU, PENNY!
YEAH... I CAN SEE WHY YOU FEEL THAT WAY.

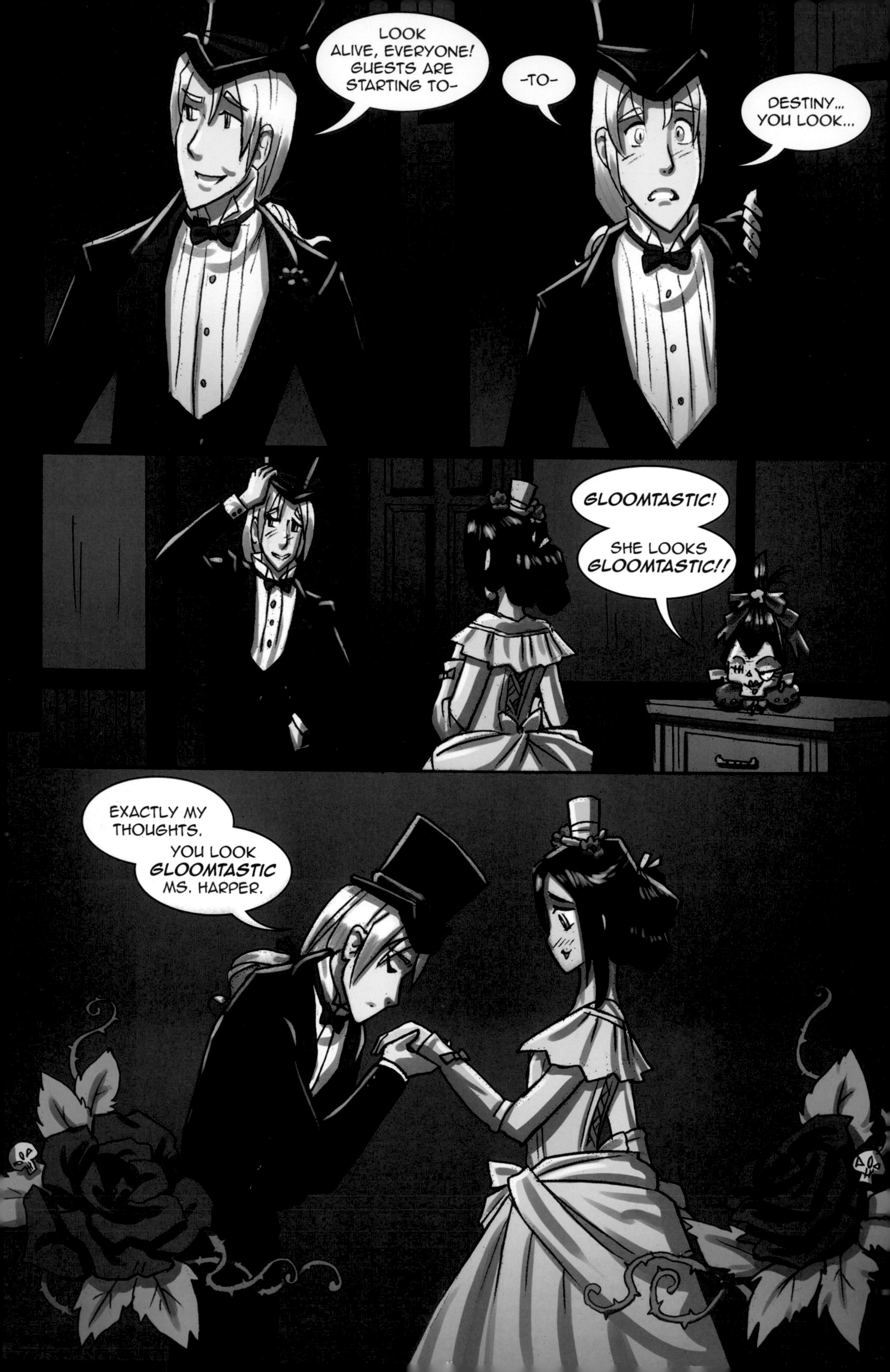

LOOK ALIVE, EVERYONE! GUESTS ARE STARTING TO-
-TO-
DESTINY... YOU LOOK...
GLOOMTASTIC!
SHE LOOKS GLOOMTASTIC!!
EXACTLY MY THOUGHTS. YOU LOOK GLOOMTASTIC MS. HARPER.

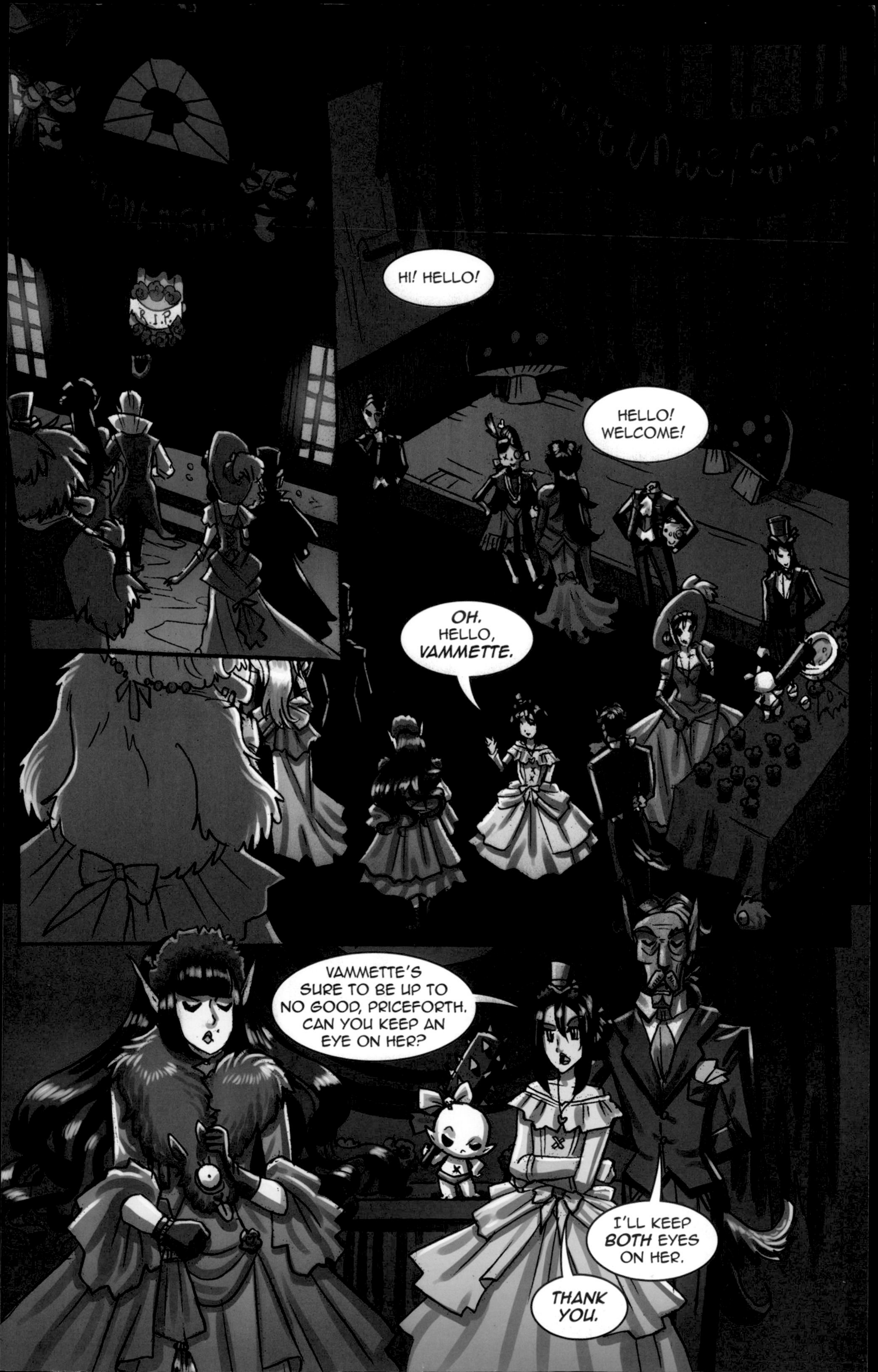
HI! HELLO!
HELLO! WELCOME!
OH. HELLO, VAMMETTE.
VAMMETTE'S SURE TO BE UP TO NO GOOD, PRICEFORTH. CAN YOU KEEP AN EYE ON HER?
I'LL KEEP BOTH EYES ON HER.
THANK YOU.

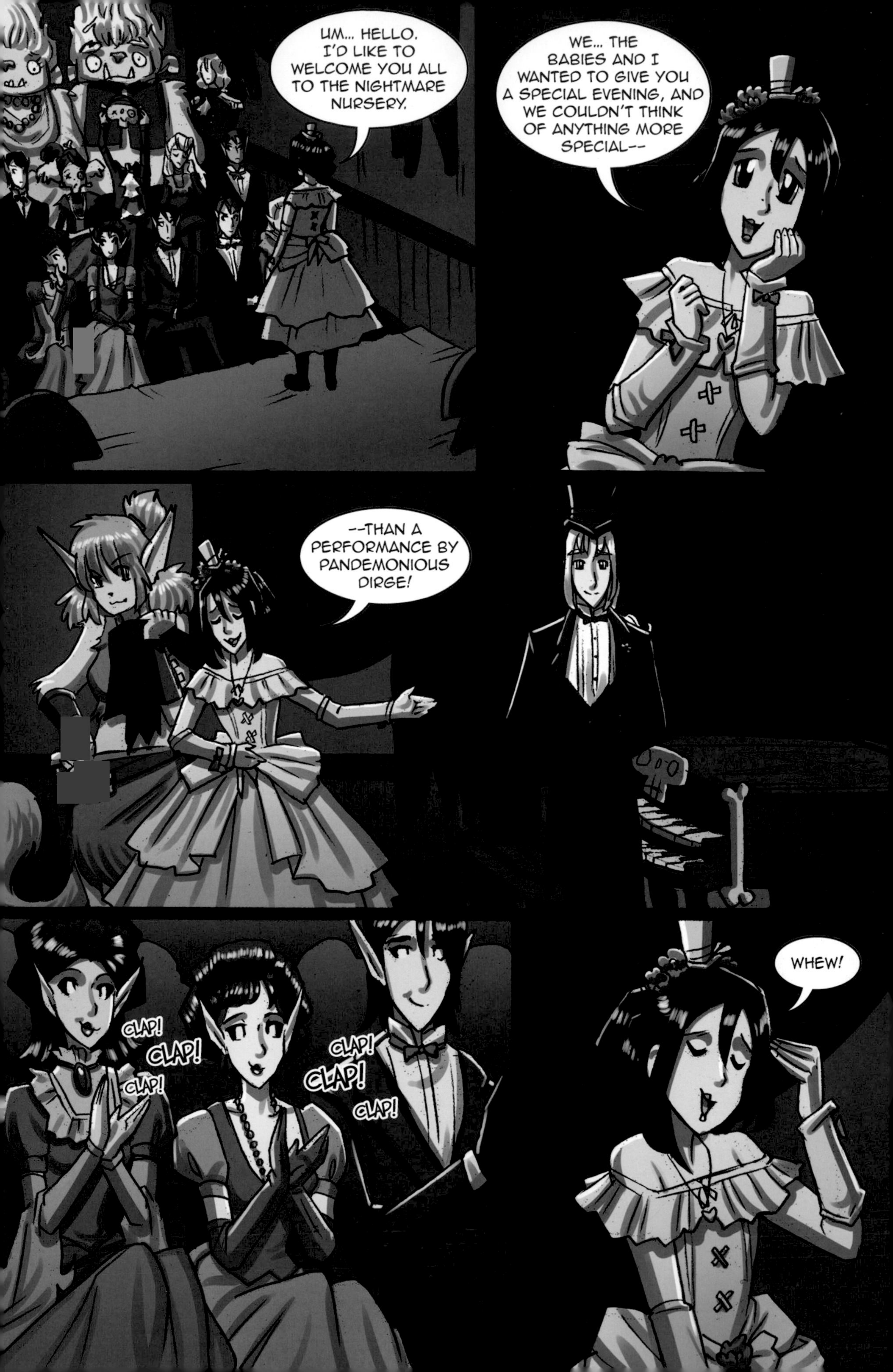
UM... HELLO. I'D LIKE TO WELCOME YOU ALL TO THE NIGHTMARE NURSERY.
WE... THE BABIES AND I WANTED TO GIVE YOU A SPECIAL EVENING, AND WE COULDN'T THINK OF ANYTHING MORE SPECIAL--
--THAN A PERFORMANCE BY PANDEMONIOUS DIRGE!
CLAP! CLAP! CLAP!
CLAP! CLAP! CLAP!
WHEW!

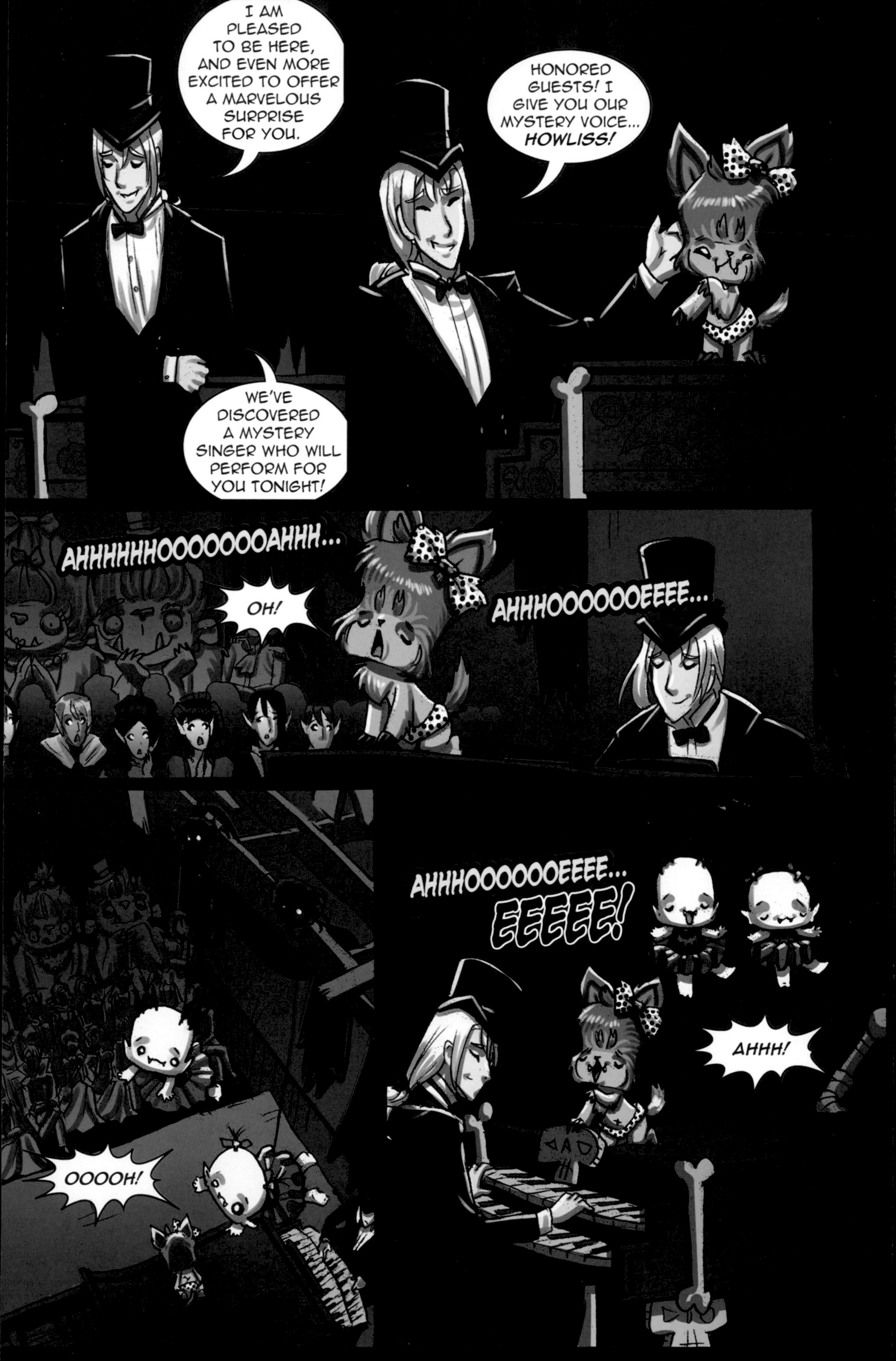

I AM PLEASED TO BE HERE, AND EVEN MORE EXCITED TO OFFER A MARVELOUS SURPRISE FOR YOU.
WE'VE DISCOVERED A MYSTERY SINGER WHO WILL PERFORM FOR YOU TONIGHT!
HONORED GUESTS! I GIVE YOU OUR MYSTERY VOICE... HOWLISS!
AHHHHHHOOOOOOOAHHH...
OH!
AHHHOOOOOOEEEE...
OOOOH!
AHHHOOOOOOEEEE... EEEEE!
AHHH!

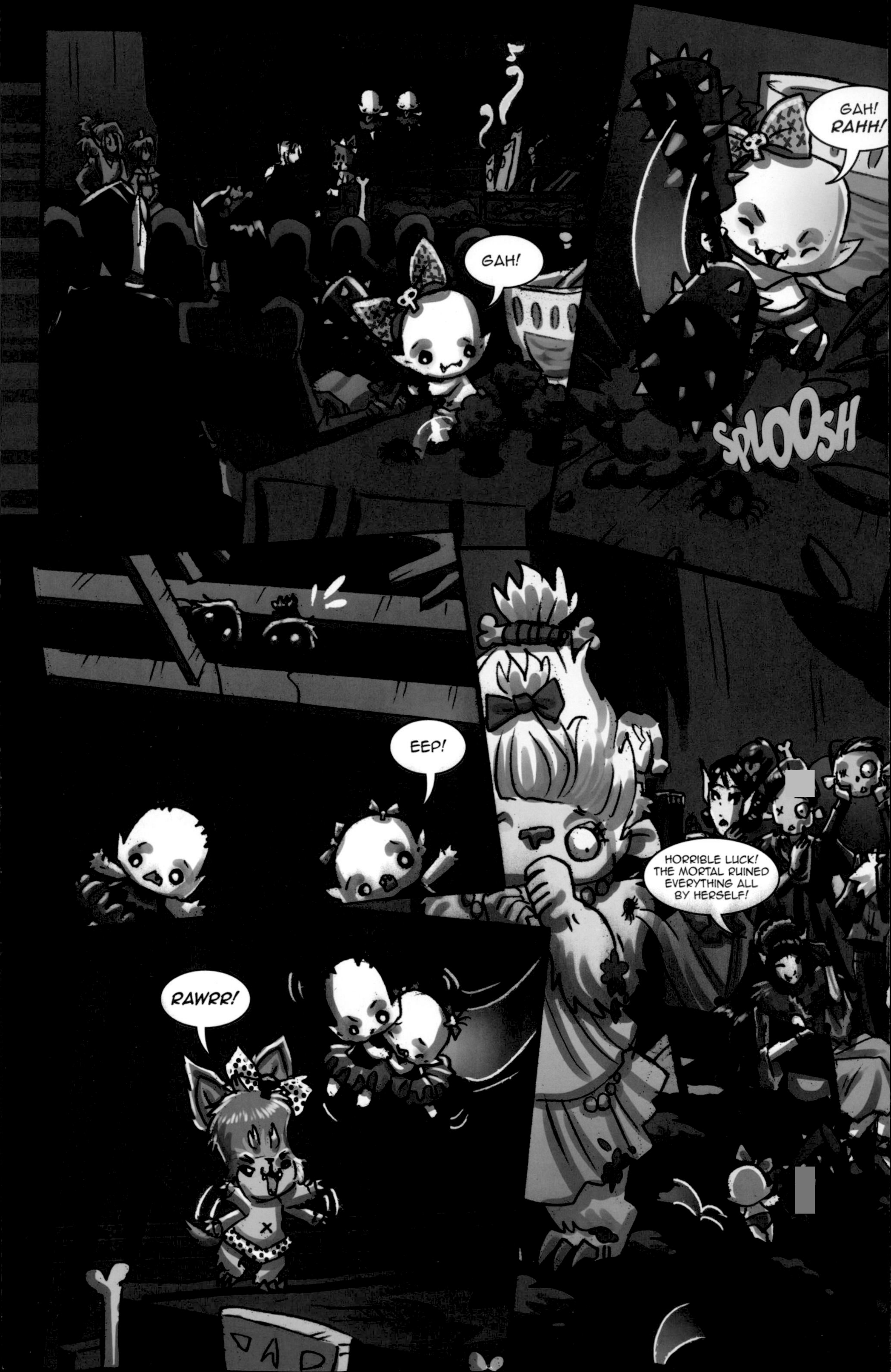
GAH!
GAH! RAHH!
SPLOOSH
EEP!
HORRIBLE LUCK! THE MORTAL RUINED EVERYTHING ALL BY HERSELF!
RAWRR!

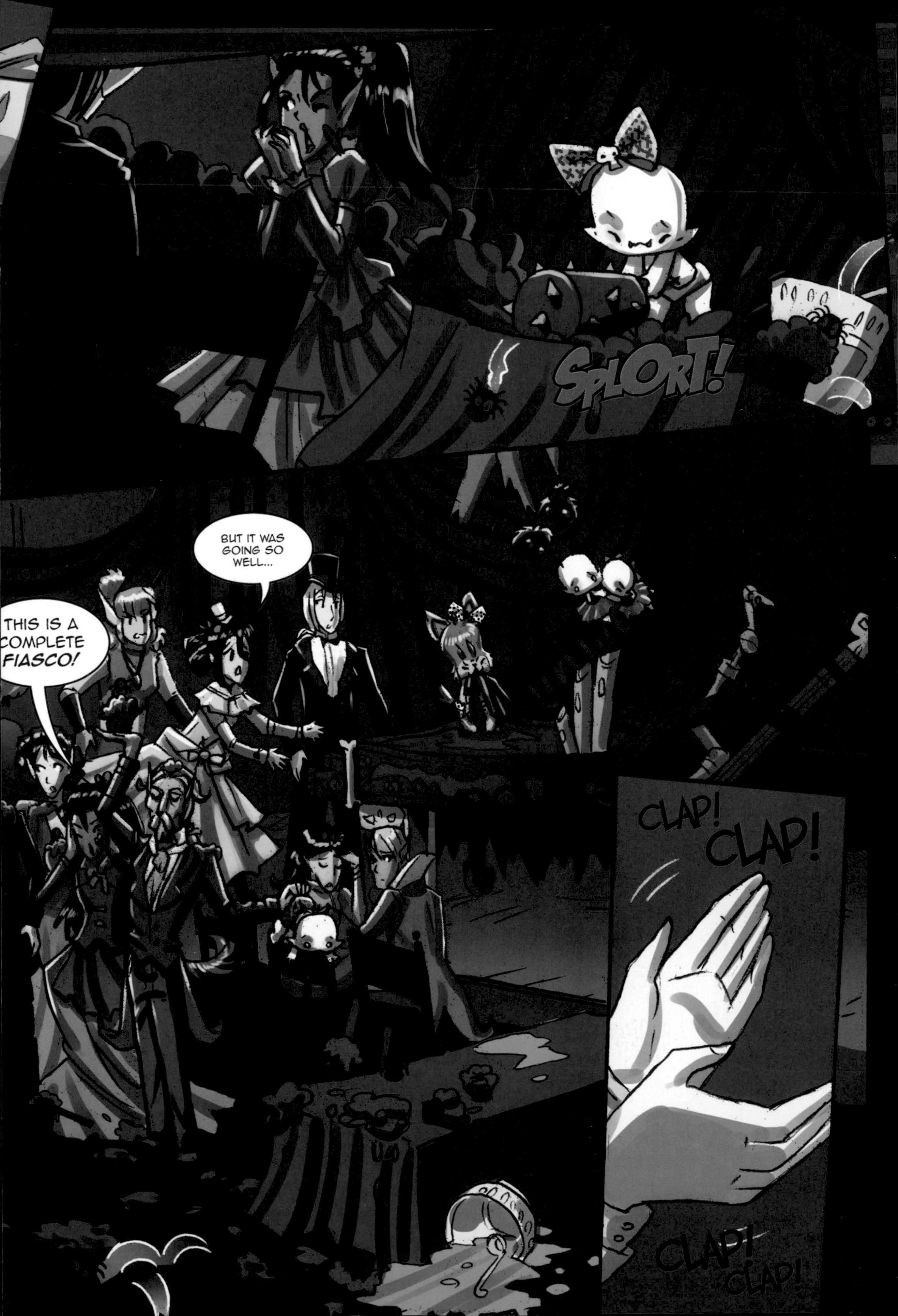

SPLORT!
BUT IT WAS GOING SO WELL...
THIS IS A COMPLETE *FIASCO!*
CLAP! CLAP!
CLAP! CLAP!

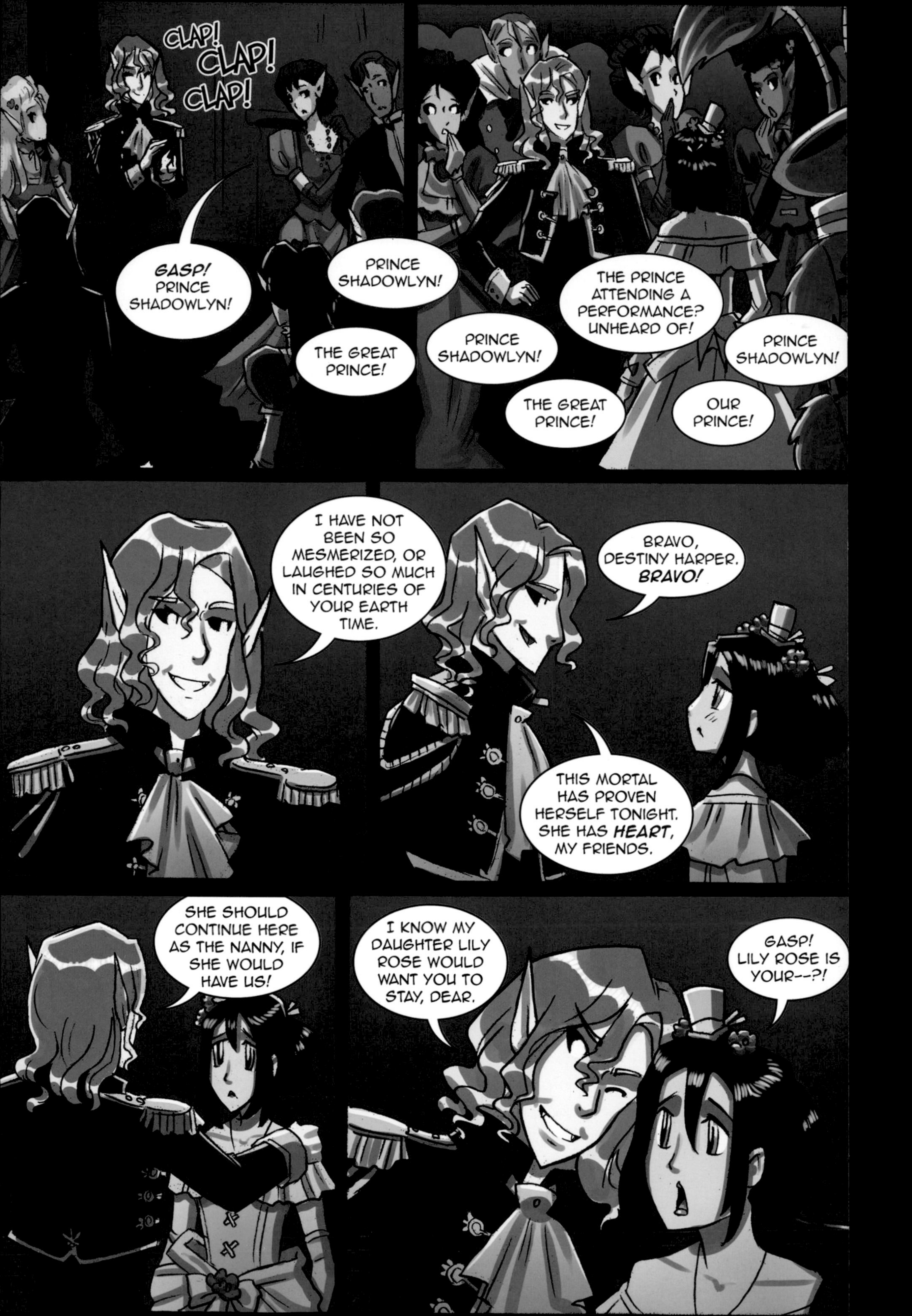
CLAP! CLAP! CLAP!
GASP! PRINCE SHADOWLYN!
PRINCE SHADOWLYN!
THE GREAT PRINCE!
PRINCE SHADOWLYN!
THE PRINCE ATTENDING A PERFORMANCE? UNHEARD OF!
THE GREAT PRINCE!
PRINCE SHADOWLYN!
OUR PRINCE!
I HAVE NOT BEEN SO MESMERIZED, OR LAUGHED SO MUCH IN CENTURIES OF YOUR EARTH TIME.
BRAVO, DESTINY HARPER. BRAVO!
THIS MORTAL HAS PROVEN HERSELF TONIGHT. SHE HAS HEART, MY FRIENDS.
SHE SHOULD CONTINUE HERE AS THE NANNY, IF SHE WOULD HAVE US!
I KNOW MY DAUGHTER LILY ROSE WOULD WANT YOU TO STAY, DEAR.
GASP! LILY ROSE IS YOUR--?!

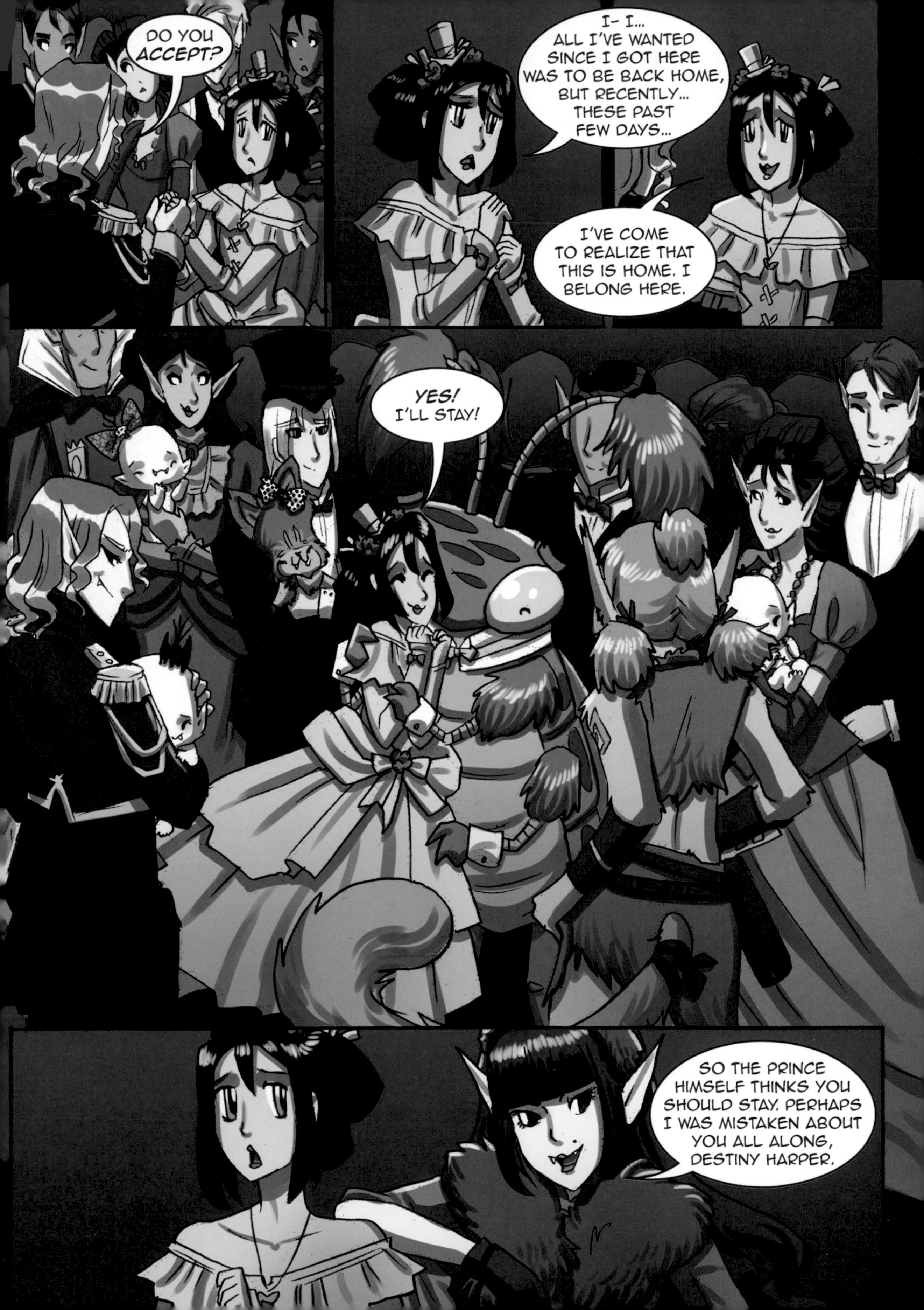
DO YOU ACCEPT?
I– I... ALL I'VE WANTED SINCE I GOT HERE WAS TO BE BACK HOME, BUT RECENTLY... THESE PAST FEW DAYS...
I'VE COME TO REALIZE THAT THIS IS HOME. I BELONG HERE.
YES! I'LL STAY!
SO THE PRINCE HIMSELF THINKS YOU SHOULD STAY. PERHAPS I WAS MISTAKEN ABOUT YOU ALL ALONG, DESTINY HARPER.

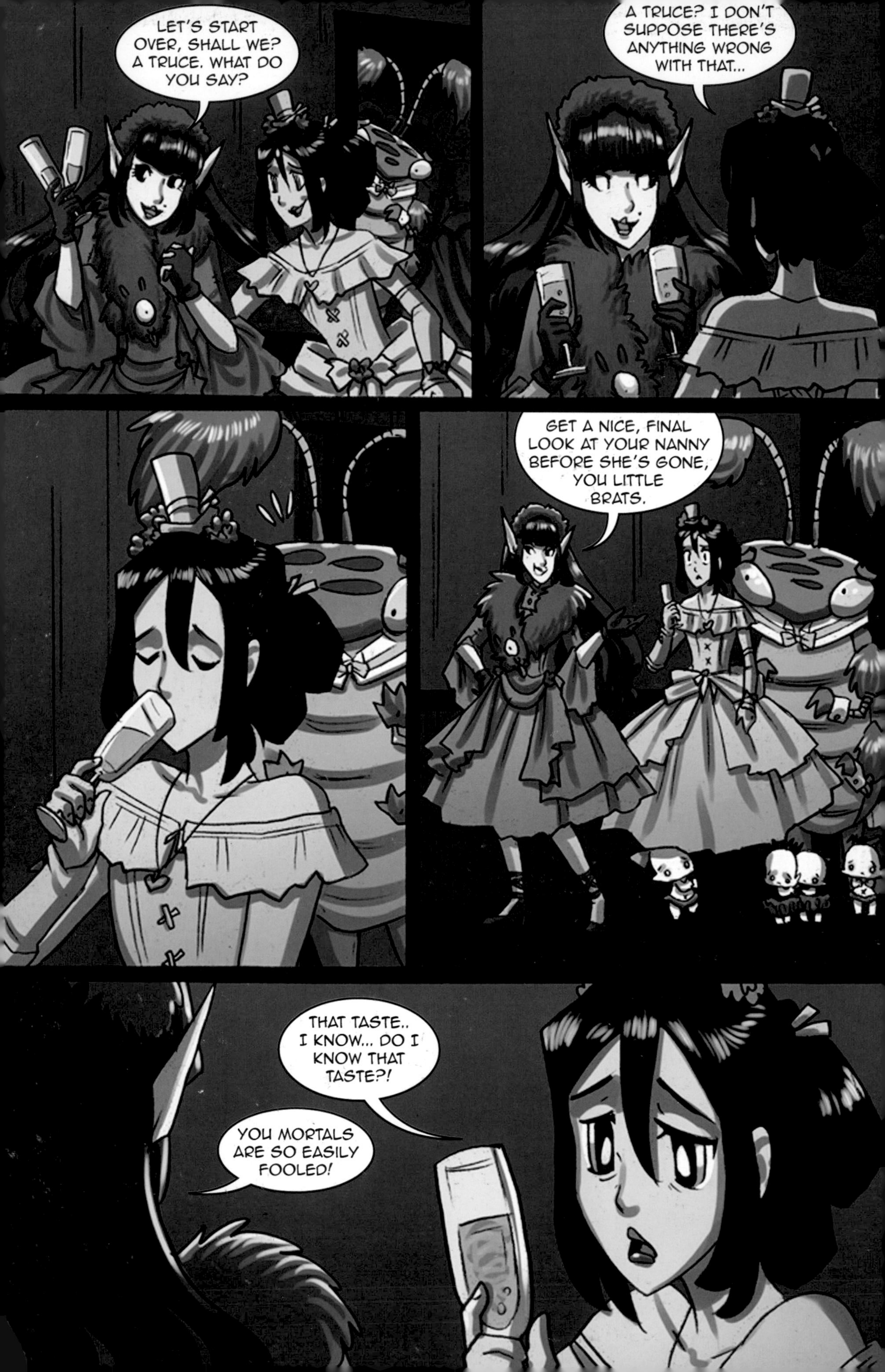
LET'S START OVER, SHALL WE? A TRUCE. WHAT DO YOU SAY?
A TRUCE? I DON'T SUPPOSE THERE'S ANYTHING WRONG WITH THAT...
GET A NICE, FINAL LOOK AT YOUR NANNY BEFORE SHE'S GONE, YOU LITTLE BRATS.
THAT TASTE.. I KNOW... DO I KNOW THAT TASTE?!
YOU MORTALS ARE SO EASILY FOOLED!

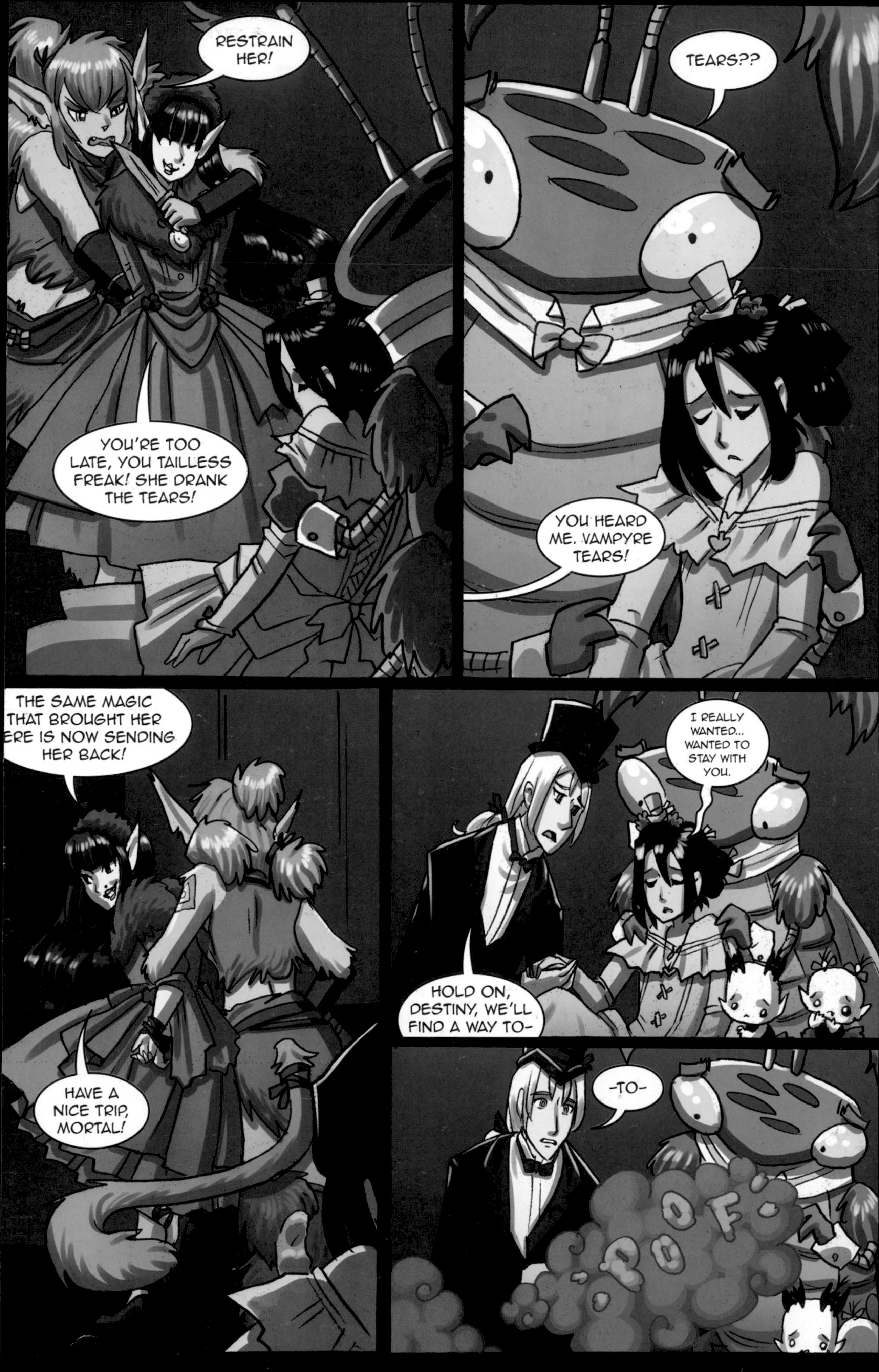
RESTRAIN HER!
YOU'RE TOO LATE, YOU TAILLESS FREAK! SHE DRANK THE TEARS!
TEARS??
YOU HEARD ME. VAMPYRE TEARS!
THE SAME MAGIC THAT BROUGHT HER ERE IS NOW SENDING HER BACK!
HAVE A NICE TRIP, MORTAL!
I REALLY WANTED... WANTED TO STAY WITH YOU.
HOLD ON, DESTINY, WE'LL FIND A WAY TO-
-TO-

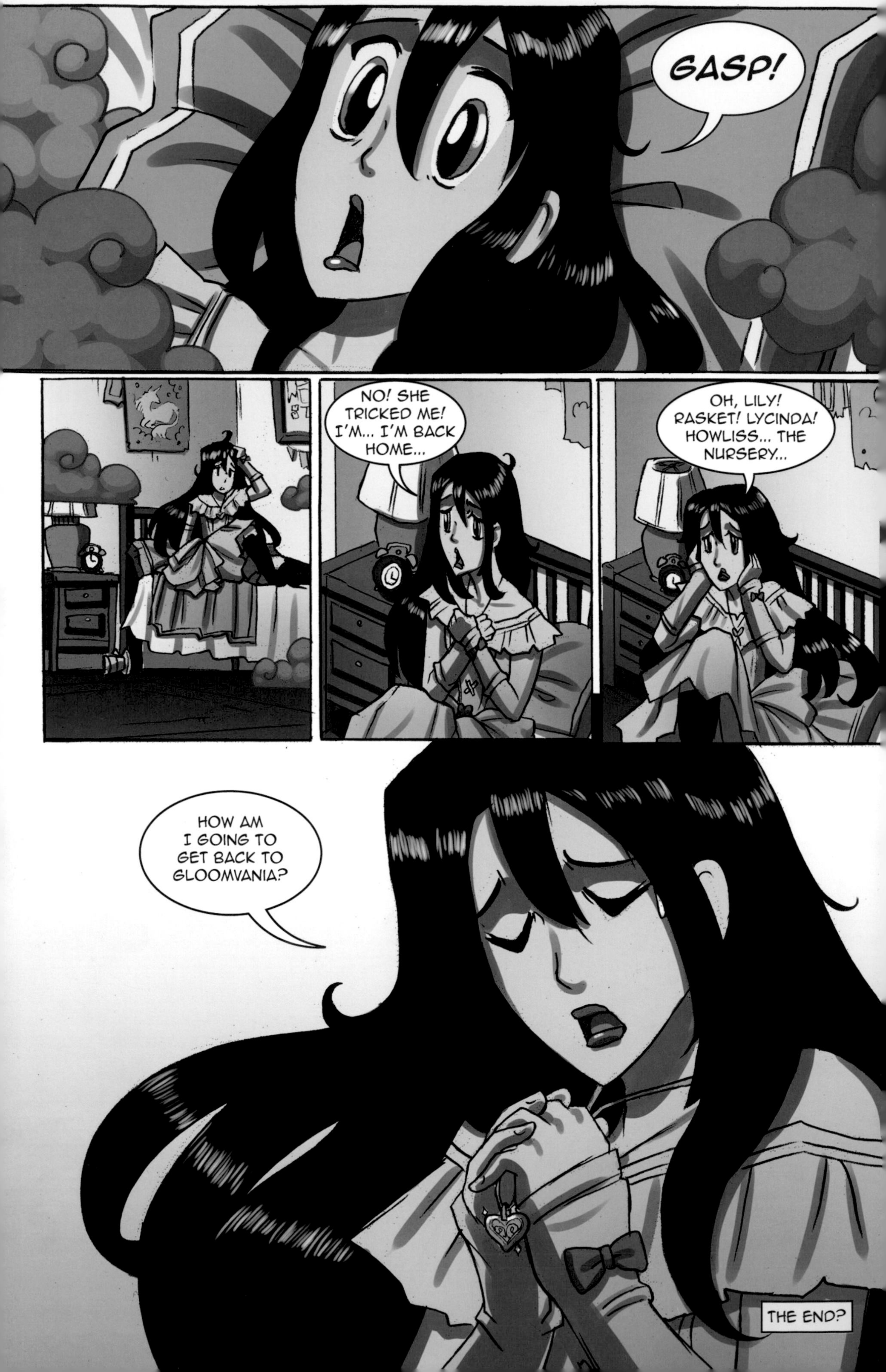
GASP!
NO! SHE TRICKED ME! I'M... I'M BACK HOME...
OH, LILY! RASKET! LYCINDA! HOWLISS... THE NURSERY...
HOW AM I GOING TO GET BACK TO GLOOMVANIA?
THE END?